D0091759

ERICH HACKL was born in 1954 in Steyr, Austria. His novels and short stories have been translated into English, Spanish, French and Czech.

THE WEDDING IN AUSCHWITZ

An Incident

ERICH HACKL

Translated by Martin Chalmers

Powell River Public Library

A complete catalogue record for this book can be obtained from
the British Library on request

The right of Erich Hackl to be identified as the author of this
work has been asserted by him in accordance with the Copyright,
Designs and Patents Act 1988

Copyright © 2002 Diogenes Verlag AG Zürich
Translation copyright © 2009 Martin Chalmers

All rights reserved. No part of this book may be reproduced, stored in a
retrieval system or transmitted in any form or by any means, electronic,
mechanical, photocopying, recording or otherwise, without the prior
permission of the publisher.

First published as *Die Hochzeit von Auschwitz* in 2002
by Diogenes, Zurich

First published in 2009 by Serpent's Tail,
an imprint of Profile Books Ltd
3A Exmouth House
Pine Street
London EC1R 0JH
website: www.serpentstail.com

ISBN 978 1 85242 983 6

Designed and typeset by Sue Lamble
Printed in Great Britain by CPI Bookmarque, Croydon CR0 4TD

10 9 8 7 6 5 4 3 2 1

FSC
Mixed Sources
Product group from well-managed
forests and other controlled sources

Cert no. SGS-COC-2061
www.fsc.org
© 1996 Forest Stewardship Council

The paper this book is printed on
is certified by the © 1996 Forest
Stewardship Council A.C. (FSC).
It is ancient-forest friendly.
The printer holds FSC chain of
custody SGS-COC-2061

*I don't know the truth – to the extent
that it exists at all. Perhaps one of
the story-tellers was lying. The opposite
is also possible: that they all just
said, what they thought was true.
Or perhaps, in the natural desire to
embellish a story, they now and again
added something of their own.
Or we may suppose that the haze of
remembering is settling on the facts
and gradually distorting, transforming,
condensing the accounts of the eyewitnesses
as much as the conclusions
of the historians.*

Sergio Atzeni, 'Bakunin's Son'

1

THE THUNDERSTORM

Tonight I'll dream about Rudi Friemel. He'll have a white face, as if made of wax, and his eyes will be wide open, as if he was frightened to death. He'll be wearing thin, striped prisoner's trousers, which hide the frostbite, and a white shirt embroidered with roses. A present, from whom? He will smile, as he always smiled. I will see the dimple in his chin. He will say: All of them have forgotten me, women, friends, comrades.

Nonsense, I'll say.

Oh Marina, my spirited little sister-in-law. Do you still remember me, Rudi will reply.

He was a good lad. Car mechanic, mad about motorbikes. A committed socialist. A little bit crazy. A daredevil, foolhardy, ready for adventure. He's said to have been brave in Vienna in February '34. Then he fled to Brno. Later he fought here in Spain. What might have become of him?

Strange, that I'll dream about him. After so many years. It's not bad to dream of the dead. But why didn't he appear to me before?

Shall I tell his story? Do you want to hear it? I'm warning you: There are only fragments of his life, and in my head they don't add up to a clear picture. The years fly past, and when one looks back, it's too late to separate imagination and reality. It would be better if you ask others about him. Although they won't be able to tell you much either. Is anybody at all still alive, of those who knew him? So many were killed. And those who weren't killed, died in bed, as people should. And those who were neither killed, nor died in bed, can't remember, because they don't want to remember. But even among those who don't want to remember, you won't find anyone any more who knew him.

Friemel. Edeltrude Friemel. Trude. I'm not related to any Rudi Friemel. But in this building, on staircase 7, there's someone who's called that. How old will he be, thirty-two, thirty-five? More like thirty-two, and his father is getting on for sixty. As far as I know, they don't have a phone.

– There's no Rudolf in our family. Hasn't been in a hundred and fifty years. Twenty-eight Friemels, and not a single Rudolf. I'm interested in genealogy, that's why. I would be interested to know whether he was born in Vienna. Because all my Friemels are from Silesia.

– Friemel, Maria. Had her phone disconnected from 30th June.

– No, Therese. Therese Friemel. I don't know any Rudolf Friemel. I can't know every Friemel, can I? Have you tried in Graz? There's supposed to be another family by the name of Friemel there.

– Friemel or Frieml. Or Frimmel. Spain, France, Poland? Look, I'm not a travel agency.

- I vaguely remember a Friemel. Though I didn't meet him

myself. But his name was often mentioned, at secret meetings with youth leaders of the Revolutionary Socialists. We met in the street to agree joint campaigns, an illegal demonstration on the 1st of May or scattering leaflets on the anniversary of the February Uprising. The name Friemel often came up in that context. We knew that he existed. He's knocking around somewhere in Favoriten. Sixty-six years ago.

– One moment, and I've got him. Freytag, Friedmann, Friedrich, Friemel. Everything I could find out about him is in the file-index box. In Spain he was with the signals, laying cables for the lines of communication. Lineman, it was called. But I only got to know him in France, in the camp. He never made a bad impression on me. On the contrary, he was a good man, and quite a lad as well.

– A ladies' man, I would say. A woman for every day of the week. I don't know what they saw in him. Perhaps it was his determination, courage matched with innocence, the dedication to a cause which he saw as right. Or they saw a sign branded on his forehead or between his eyes that we men missed. At any rate they flocked to him like moths to the flame.

– The name's like a red rag to me even now. Friemel cost me sleepless nights. For hours I kept watch on his flat, his father's flat and the flat of his sister, who was married to a man called Korvas, another radical. Nothing. The next day I found out, he's been seen here and there. So he was in the flat after all! He played cat and mouse with me. But sooner or later every one gets caught in the trap. The arm of the law is long.

– He was my father. I hardly knew him. The few memories have faded. But somewhere there must still be a shoe box lying around, it was passed on to me from my grandfather. There are letters and photos in it. Not many, as far as I could see when I took a quick look at it. My grandfather's second wife had died, the flat had to be cleared, the house management was insistent. To be honest, up to now I haven't been able to bring myself to open the box.

Today I will also dream about my sister. For years I don't dream at all, or I only dream silly stuff which I've already forgotten when I wake up. But mostly I don't even get round to dreaming, because the man beside me gabbles night after night. In his sleep he makes big speeches. Fernando, I say, will you please be quiet! When there's peace at last, I'm bound to get a poke in the ribs, Marina, you're snoring, says Fernando and rolls over, but I'm lying awake and can't fall asleep until morning. And now what I want is this: two nights in a row with no blathering and no poke in the ribs, and one night Rudi appears, the next night Margarita. I think she'll appear to me in a dream because she's jealous. It's not me, it's you that's jealous, she'll say. Don't talk nonsense, I'll reply.

Poor Marga.

The birth certificate, made out by the Parish of the Holy Family in Neu-Ottakring. According to it he was born on 11th May 1907 at 9 Habichergasse, Vienna, and the following day christened Rudolf Adolf. His father is given as Clemens Friemel, Roman Catholic, plasterer, born 21.12.1881 in Prague. Mother: Stefanie, née Spitzer, Roman Catholic, maidservant, born 20.12.1882 in Vienna.

His school leaving certificate, made out by the three class Vocational School for Mechanics in Vienna, VI District, 87 Mollardgasse.

The certificate according to which on 4th July 1925 he passed his apprentices' final examination with good marks.

His licence to drive motor vehicles with internal combustion engines and motorcycles with sidecars.

Testimonials from the companies Steyrer Mill, Associated Dairies, OEWA (water piping), New Vienna Daily and Viennese Pork Butchers Production Company. According to them he carried out all his work conscientiously, but unfortunately has to be made redundant because of a lack of orders.

The photographs. First of all a girl in a summer dress with bangles and a headband. My aunt. She has dark eyes. Is she smiling? I doubt it. There are flowers in her lap. Forsythia or delphiniums. I can't make out much. The photo is rather underexposed. Written on the back is: 'Your sister Steferl. 17/XI.1923. 1st Prize Beauty Contest'.

Then three pictures of my father, taken in a photographic studio. I do actually think I look like him. Aside from the fact that I'm taller and sturdier and much older than he was then; also, apart from the fact that I've got my mother's round chin – the high forehead, the thick, wavy hair are his. Except his eyes are different. Not arrogant, but somehow challenging, headstrong, obstinate. A vigorous young man in a suit and tie. Once he's sitting, once he's standing, once he's bare-headed, once he's wearing a hat and carrying a walking stick. That was in May 1927, on his twentieth birthday. I don't know what bothers me about the pictures. Is it the smart clothes or the artificial lighting or the oriental background? The way he seems to freeze, or the certainty that I'll never catch up with him. In the third picture he's wearing a cardigan. I like him better there, even if he's putting on a serious face. He doesn't seem so cold. He could accept me the way I am.

My mother. Snapshot. She looks pretty exhausted. But when she was young she was quite cheerful. She laughed, went out a lot, she also played in a mandolin orchestra. Later on she didn't laugh much.

Ten or twelve poems, partly handwritten, partly typed. I didn't know that he wrote poems as well. I don't usually read poems. But I like these. They rhyme and they're humorous. Not all of them, some are serious. One about the passing of the seasons, one about a poor orphan child, who ends up a prostitute, one about an absent love, two about his longing to see me: 'My Little Son', 'To Norbert!' He must have written those in exile. So he did think of me. 'Waking, dreaming, I always hear your childlike laughter crystal clear.' Then there are political poems about the people in chains and about the struggle for freedom and the victorious unfurling of the red flag.

Red is still my favourite colour, I'll say to him. Because I was born a Red, at the time of the Great October Revolution, and I'll go to my grave a Red. I don't take any credit for that, it simply happened, I didn't choose my parents and my circumstances.

My mother was from Madrid. Her father was José Rey, an important figure in the Socialist Party, their number two after Pablo Iglesias. He died young. My grandmother too. At five my mother was an orphan. She sewed shirts. She learned her craft from an aunt.

My father grew up on Minorca. The Ferrers had Jewish ancestors. So at some time they had been persecuted. That didn't stop them running after every cowl and cassock and making common cause with the moneybags on the island. It was my father who stepped out of line. At seventeen he came to Madrid to study. But before he enrolled at university, a post in the customs became vacant. His application was successful and he took up the position. He paid for his studies with it. Because his parents, who were raking in the money with their pharmacy, didn't forgive him. They didn't slip him a single duro, because of his revolutionary views, so different from theirs, and because he gave every church a wide berth. While he was studying he lived in the Calle Montera, where the prostitutes stand around now, in a pension in which my mother washed dishes. That's how they got to know each other. My mother was then eight years old.

Nine or ten years later he knocked on a shop door in the Calle Encomienda, corner of Mesón de Paredes. Not a good area either, not even today. The anarchists held their meetings there. My mother was friends with the sister of an anarchist. And by chance she was visiting on the evening of the meeting and my father was there, too, and they immediately clicked. Like you and Margarita, I'll say to Rudi. My father was nine years older than my mother. Rudi was also a bit older than Margarita.

What's your name, asked my father.

Rosario.

Oh really? I once knew a Rosario.

That was me.

That's how it all began.

It began with my parents getting to know each other after the Social Democratic Party May Day rally. That was in 1930, in the Prater. My mother's name was Pauline, but everyone called her Paula. She supported the party, only she wasn't as committed as he was. He was a monus driver, he delivered newspapers. A monus was a motorcycle with three wheels, two at the front, one at the back, at the front there was a box for the newspapers. He was only employed by the day. In between he was frequently unemployed. My mother was a salesgirl at the Hammer Bakeries. Then she was laid off too. I remember we once collected the unemployment benefit, it was twelve schillings. On the way home on the tram we lost the money. My mother was in despair. Her sister, she was unmarried, helped us out then. She also helped out otherwise. He was never there of course. If he was there for once, there was no reason for me to be afraid. He was always nice to me. Sometimes he did speak more sharply, but he never hit me. On the other hand he didn't do anything for me. My mother had to bear the whole burden, he never supported her financially. She didn't attach great importance to that anyway.

My mother the daughter of a leading socialist, my father an anarchist, then a communist. We came from radical stock. I was just fourteen when I went to my first meeting. That was 1931 or 1932. More like '32, January 1932. In those days the workers' leaders still had a different way of explaining the class struggle. Blunt, and perhaps a little naive. They laid into the bourgeoisie, who were to be exterminated. They said, the bourgeois can be recognised by his hat (and I got a fright, because my father wore a hat), he can be recognised by his walking stick (and again I got a fright, because my father carried a walking stick), he can be recognised by his tie (and yes! my father also wore a tie). They said the bourgeois sucked the workers' blood. I was paralysed, completely paralysed. I couldn't say a word. I didn't dare look at anyone, I was shaking with fear, in case someone said, look, that's the daughter of a bloodsucker sitting there, beat her to death.

In my grandfather's shoe box I found a report of the Federal Police Headquarters Vienna, in which a whole number of convictions are listed: Juvenile Court Vienna, 19.5.1924, in accordance with section 460 Criminal Code 5 days close arrest suspended; District Court I, 16.7.1926, in accordance with section 431 of the Criminal Code 48 hours arrest; Provincial Court I, 6.4.1933, in accordance with section 197, 199d Criminal Code 14 days close arrest, suspended until 6th April 1935 to be placed on the record; District Court X, 2.1.1934, in accordance with section 411 Criminal Code 16 schillings, in case of non-payment 24 hours arrest. It is also noted, that on 21st November 1932 my father was arrested after a charge was brought of offending public decency by insulting a passer-by, who was reading a National Socialist poster. He was released by the police station after notification of the charge. Friemel, it is stated, was wearing the badge of the Social Democratic Party while the person bringing the charge was wearing no party badge.

I hadn't known anything about that. In fact I only knew about one previous conviction: My father had built a motorcycle and wanted to take it for a test ride. He made a number plate from a piece of cardboard. A policeman stopped and charged him. I think that was already after I was born, whereas the accident happened before that, 1930 or '31. My parents went on a motorbike trip. In Styria he failed to see road works which had no warning lights. They had a bad crash, my mother had a fracture at the base of the skull and knocked out all her front teeth. So she already got a bridge at the age of twenty-four, she had it till she was sixty, only then did the dentist fit her with a denture.

When she got out of hospital, the doctor said: Now just you don't ride pillion on a motorcycle any more, and she answered:

Take a look out of the window, there he is already. So she got on the motorcycle behind him again, and they roared off, home to Favoriten.

Favoriten was a hard place for anyone who had to maintain law and order. It was either brawling and boozing or it was politics and shooting. The result was the same: out of the station house and off to the scene of the action, taking statements, examining witnesses, carrying out arrests. There were always insults and jeers. The witnesses had seen nothing, the delinquents resisted arrest or evaded it by taking flight. Physical violence was nothing out of the ordinary. Mistelbacher, get lost, or I'll cut your throat. More than once my cap was knocked off my head. When I bent down, they put a foot on it. And grinned. There were twenty of them and two of us. Even the children were stirred up against us. And the females. The old people. The unemployed. The brick workers from Oberlaa. Red riff-raff, and the Party bosses in city hall protected them. At the weekends the Social Democratic Schutzbund held its marches, carried out manoeuvres on the Laaerberg, in uniform, with weapons, and all we could do was watch. But in '33 the tables were turned. Dollfuss got rid of parliament, introduced the death sentence, banned the Schutzbund. We knew now it was time to crack down hard. They're in a corner. We have to wear them down. Then we got the order to locate the places where their weapons were hidden. In the party's section houses we dug through the coal in the cellars, again and again. Of course we didn't find anything. Black from head to toe we withdrew after hours of searching, laughed and jibed at. Well, Mistelbacher, been cleaning the chimney. Then when things were getting too hot for them, they struck. But the forces of law and order were on their guard. Then they were laughing on the other side of their faces.

Friemel was one of the ringleaders. A particularly rabble-rousing individual, but one, I'll say that for him, who fought fair and square. There were others who conformed. Who talked big and then had their tail between their legs. No one can accuse him of that. Nevertheless by rights he should have hung. Because in the course of the fighting on 12th February 1934 as leader of an armed group of the Schutzbund he fired on my colleague, Department Inspector Schuster. That was in Kudlichgasse, at about five pm, outside Sobotka's hairdresser's shop. A bullet in the abdomen at very close range. A second member of the security forces, Senior Constable Reimann, I think, got away with two bullets in his thigh. But Schuster died the next day. From that you can see that the Reds stopped at nothing. Friemel avoided arrest by taking flight. He crossed over to Czechoslovakia and conducted a lively correspondence from there, which was partly intercepted, partly handed over to us by the addressees. His wife is also supposed to have made a letter available to the authorities. I don't know whether that's true. I was aware, however, that the Friemel couple were not on the best of terms. There was also a young woman in the district, who was said to be Friemel's lover. Whether she was, I don't know. At any rate we found illegal propaganda material at her place.

We didn't catch Friemel until the end of August. That was lucky for him. The political situation had changed by then, examples had been made, the main worry was no longer the Socialists, but the Nazis, who were getting stronger all the time. Apart from which Friemel defended himself very skilfully in court. He was certainly self-assured, one has to grant him that, and that was something the judge evidently liked. The charge of murder was dropped and so he got away with a prison sentence for riot and malicious damage. The trial caused a bit of a stir. I remember that the night before we detained several Communists who had scattered leaflets in Favoriten: 'Save Schutzbund leader Rudolf Friemel from life imprisonment!', 'Down with Italian Fascism!'

I believe that after sentence was pronounced Friemel was put in Stein Prison and transferred from there to Wöllersdorf. I don't know what happened to him after that. Whether later on he was for the Nazis or against them... He wasn't a Yid. Personally I got on well with the Nazis. I joined them, after all.

When my sister and I were still children, my father withdrew to the kitchen every lunchtime with a couple of workers. There they alternately read *Das Kapital* and the Bible. And on the even days he interpreted Marx and on the odd ones the Bible.

My father was a biologist and a doctor. He had studied both, and then he was about to graduate in astronomy as well. He only practised as a doctor during the war, from two to six in the afternoon. His real field was biology. He specialised in single-celled organisms. Heaven knows why he found them so interesting. Polycellular organisms bored him. But if it had only one cell, then he dropped everything else. He travelled a great deal, to England, to Germany, to the Red Sea. Even to India. All because of his beloved single-celled organisms. He also wrote many books. The Institute of Oceanography offered him a chair, that's why we moved to Barcelona.

He had a worldwide reputation as a biologist. Years after his death Hitler requested a photo of him, and my grandfather sent one to Berlin. A picture of a Spanish anarchist and Communist, and one with Jewish ancestors as well, hanging in the Nazis' Natural History Museum! I'd rather not imagine what he would have said about that.

My mother never went to school. She was very conscientious, she was a good worker, but not terribly bright, to be honest. She was a bit simple, with all due respect. I remember that one day my father explained the heavens to her. He tried to teach her that the moon orbits the earth, that it's far away and that it's very large. And she says, how large, like this wash tub? A grown woman! She was very shy, easily scared, because she had a very hard time as a child. Not later on.

My sister took after her. Margarita was timid, unsure of herself, very feminine. She left every decision to others. Although she could be quite obstinate. What she set her mind on, she got. Even if in a roundabout way.

I think my father put politics even before his family. My mother didn't go along with that. So they drifted apart. My father also had the reputation of being a bit of a ladies' man, allegedly he had relationships on the side, and that's how the hostility between my mother and my grandfather arose. They didn't talk to each other any more. She blamed him for my father being unfaithful, and for introducing other women to him. I don't know to what extent that's true.

My grandfather lived opposite us on Ernst Ludwig Gasse. We could look across from our flat. And my father and my grandfather had arranged that in the event of a house search or an arrest my grandfather would put something in the window. I don't know what any more. And I remember that my father got up once, he's just pulled on his trousers, looks across and shouts: Damn it all, they're here! He picked up his belt and struck the bed with it. That stuck in my mind.

Otherwise it's only fragments that occur to me. Early in the morning, when I had got up, the first thing he asked was: Where's your handkerchief? It was my duty, as it were, to observe the proprieties. I had a pair of pyjamas with a breast pocket, and in the breast pocket there had to be a handkerchief. I have one of his letters, in it he writes to my mother, she shouldn't overfeed me, she should see to it that I eat only as much as I need, and he gives her various instructions, as to how I'm supposed to behave, that I should stick at gymnastics, greet loudly, walk with my head up.

My father came home just once more, and they argued, argued more and more violently, until he said to my mother, I'm going to shoot you! And she was derisive, yes, with a sausage.

He stayed with us for two days, then he was gone for good. I think, that was early '38, a couple of weeks before the Germans marched in.

My brother Paco and I were very politicised. Not Margarita; she was more like our mother, reserved and a bit anxious. Paco had studied geology. And I wanted to be a teacher. Then the Civil War began. Paco had very bad asthma. That didn't stop him from going to the front with a militia unit. Later he was employed by the Soviet news agency. He read all the Spanish newspapers and chose the articles which were to be printed in Russia. Margarita had gone to commercial college. She could type very fast. She didn't have many skills apart from that. She had trouble with numbers. She was in despair sometimes, I'm no good for anything, I'm stupid, but no, Marga, you have other aptitudes, to each according to his talents.

I wanted to work for the resistance to Franco. So after war broke out I took a post as teacher in the Orfelinato Rivas, in

Barcelona. Before the war the Rivas had been an orphanage, then it was turned into a military hospital, intended for militiamen with head wounds. I worked there every day, with the surgeon Dr Ley. Many patients had lost their eyesight. They tried not to show their feelings, but I knew what state they were in. They were desperate and were only waiting for the opportunity to take their own lives. They needed something that connected them to the world. I was able to find a teacher for the blind, who taught them braille. So they learned to cope by themselves. While they were practising how to make out the letters of the alphabet by touch, I attended to the others, who could see, but were blind in a different way. So many of the militiamen were illiterate. So very many. Later, in prison, I once again taught others reading and writing. This time my charges were women, prisoners like myself. Spain, this godforsaken country, was cursed by the scourge of ignorance.

Margarita worked as my father's secretary. In the afternoon he was at his practice, but in the morning he pursued his researches. He also gave some lectures. His institute was by the harbour, and he took Margarita with him, she was his favourite daughter. She was shaking with fear, because the harbour was bombed every day, but not my hospital, because it was up on the hill.

In Spain it was only in the first few months after the outbreak of the war that there were women soldiers. At the end of '36 with the raising of the regular People's Army that was over and done with. Women were not mobilised, were not called up, were not sent to the front, even those who insisted on it. The right decision, no doubt. I only need to think what it's like in the trenches. Awful. I don't just mean the lice. The trench is your home and your toilet and your bed and your laundry. But you've never got yourself to yourself. There's always someone watching you. You squat down, crap, and then you take a shovel and throw the crap out. That's life in the trenches. If your section of the front is quiet, you look for lice. You can't wash yourself, because there's no water, unless you go to fetch it at night. If you're unlucky a sniper gets you. I mean. All those songs about a wonderful soldier's life, it's all fairy tales! The wonderful soldier's life is shit. Crap. Filth. Early in the morning you get up beside your comrade, and in the evening he's gone. Dead. With his guts hanging out. Or maimed. But please, let's leave it at that. There's no need for me to talk about it. Friemel went through it too.

Margarita and me, we got to know Rudi at the same time. He had come to Spain to fight against Franco with the International Brigades. In spring '38 his battalion was on the River Ebro. One day the word came, the Mujeres Antifascistas will visit a position held by the International Brigades at Falset on the eastern front. That often happened. It was our task to entertain the soldiers, to take their minds off gloomy thoughts, to let them forget the grind of war for a couple of hours at least. My sister liked to take part in such excursions. I didn't, I hated them. It was the one and only time I went along. There must have been a hundred girls and young women, on four or five trucks. The journey was constantly interrupted. Air-raid warning, enemy fire. When we arrived the men had set a long table, with food, which they had saved for us. That made me very sad. Because they're fighting for us, don't have enough to eat, and there we come driving up from the hinterland, smart, dressed up to the nines, and let them spoil us. Yes, if we had come with rifles! If we had fought side by side with them!

There were volunteers from every country. Hungarians, Dutch, Germans, Poles, North Americans. Communication wasn't a problem. They learned Spanish very quickly. With four words they could already stick up for themselves. There was one who was constantly pulling a little dictionary out of his pocket, an Austrian, Rudi. He was the most amusing of all of them.

Of course you're glad of the visit. You're glad, if you're simply allowed to look at a woman. You're also glad about the presents they've brought, cigarettes and chocolate, although you have a bad conscience, because these presents are scarce goods, which they've perhaps done without themselves, and which are hardly to be got in the cities any more, but which you, when your unit is relieved and is being rested for a couple of days, can easily afford with the pay you've saved. You're glad and you watch and listen, and then the official part of the visit is over, and because you're still a silly lad and don't dare speak to young women, who are perhaps only waiting to be spoken to, but also perhaps, because they're engaged or even married, or because they're quick to talk back, which you like, but it also unsettles you, or because you're not a silly lad any more, but want to remain true to the girl, who in Austria or on the run somewhere else, is perhaps at this very moment thinking of you, or because you have principles which come first, namely to be alert in the struggle against Fascism, alert and disciplined, that's why you hang around for a bit after the flag has been handed over and after the anthems have been sung, smoke one of the cigarettes that have been brought, smile in embarrassment, can't stand still and, without having intended it, end up in your trench again, where you pick up the binoculars and scan the bare grey hills for Junkers and Caproni bombers, because, you tell yourself, it's better to be safe than sorry. And you hardly distinguish any more the high and the deep voices, the laughing and giggling now and then, don't even hear the engines starting up and roaring. The war has you in its grip again.

But please, let's leave it at that. Friemel went through it too.

Then at four there suddenly came the order to go into action. We had to go back. They still had time, gentlemen that they were, to help us onto the trucks. On saying goodbye Rudi embraced me. As he did so, he told me that he had fallen in love with my sister. Well, I was never at a loss for words. Aha, I said, Cupid has shot an arrow. He laughed and leafed through his dictionary. Ah you, sharp tongue, sharp tongue! I liked that very much. And I liked him immediately. Because he had a sense of humour.

Margarita was in love too. She already admitted it to me on the drive back. So Cupid had shot two arrows. One at Rudi, the other at my sister. He scored two bull's eyes. I can't think of any other explanation for a love that is kindled in the space of four hours. Although it wasn't so surprising. You were very charming, Rudi. You were also attractive. You looked like a film star. Always a smile on your lips, friendly, strong, not too tall, but not short either. Why didn't you just stay in France afterwards? You were fit, you had work, the two of you would have got by.

I didn't get to know Friemel until the International Brigades were withdrawn. That was in Bisaura de Ter. It was there, in Catalonia, that I became a functionary of the Communist Party. I had begun to organise political activity, and I encountered the Socialists and had discussions with them, with Rudi Friemel as well, he was a good lad, and an important contact. I was surprised how well he coped with the situation. We were, in fact, in a shitty position. We were the fall guys. The government of the Spanish Republic withdrew us from the front and put us before an international commission. It wanted to gain the goodwill of the democratic states: See, on our side there is no foreign intervention! Franco on the other hand was supported by Moroccan mercenaries, by Mussolini's soldiers, by the Nazi Condor Legion. It didn't work out. The foreign powers had long ago become indifferent to the struggle of the Spanish people. They were only interested in getting themselves out of a tight spot. They even closed the borders. Only Mexico was prepared to take us in, its government even sent a ship to Bordeaux, but then evidently took fright at its own courage. We didn't know what was going to happen to us. We were in correspondingly poor spirits. Even some of my own comrades lacked any kind of discipline. I tracked down one senior functionary in an attic, where he was playing cards day and night. Two others were at loggerheads over a trifle. The only concern of a fourth was that the bottle of wine in front of him was never empty. Friemel on the other hand never let things get him down. At any rate I never noticed that it did. He was always in a good mood, cheerful, almost euphoric. He was often away. When he came back, his face was glowing.

At that time we were living in the Calle Villamarí. Whenever he was in Barcelona, Rudi phoned and arranged to meet Marga. Then I had to go downstairs with her, to the next corner, where he was already waiting. I was the chaperone, so to speak. A kiss, a squeezed hand, and then I left them alone. Until nine. Because we had to be home at nine on the dot. My parents didn't have a clue.

But one day the door bell rings, my father goes to open, and Rudi's standing outside and asking him for his daughter's hand. He wanted to take Marga with him there and then.

When will that have been? The International Brigades were withdrawn from the front in the autumn. It was just before that, so in September, September '38.

My father saw him for the first time. Suddenly finds himself standing opposite a man, who's speaking broken Spanish and is already over thirty, almost ten years older than my sister. Without much ceremony he threw Rudi out.

My sister was crying. She was head over heels in love. But she was also my father's favourite child, and a father who is crazy about his daughter is hard to win round. My father's doting affection was because of my birth. Marga is fourteen months older than I am. When my mother became pregnant with me, she had to wean Marga. From then on my father gave her the bottle, night after night. So he became very attached to her. And he didn't want to give up his darling, least of all to someone he didn't know, who wanted everything at once. Yet my father had progressive views. But he was simply of a different generation. An example: On the eve of the Civil War, on 17th July 1936, I came home at five past nine instead of nine. My father hit me so hard that I was knocked right across the room. But only a day later he gives me the key to the apartment. He wanted me to go and look for my brother, at the front, behind the barricades.

My mother had no say. Absolutely none at all. That's how it was then. The men did what they liked, whenever it suited them. But the women... Well, the women! Home at nine, in bed at twelve.

It was in Alfambra, north of Teruel, very close to the front. Paseo on the main square. The lads and the girls went strolling there. One lot went anti-clockwise, the other clockwise. When they met, they shouted something to each other. That was all! Not one of the girls walked with the boys, and not one of the boys walked with the girls. Always just round in a circle. You watched them, on the main square of Alfambra.

It was in Castelserás, twelve or thirteen miles behind the front. The population welcomed the Fourth Battalion enthusiastically, it was a sensation. Foreigners! The International Brigades! Russians! There was no lack of food mind you; the whole village was collectivised, the anarchists were dominant there. Money didn't count, but the men of the Brigades could pay in pesetas. When they marched in, a woman came up to you, to you and to another, did you need quarters for the night, she can offer you a good room. You went with them. They lived in a house next to the church, the woman and her husband and two daughters, who were perhaps eighteen and twenty. The girls' bedroom was cleared for you, you set down your kit, and then the woman said: Well, you are going to honour us with your presence for a few days, my daughters will try to make the stay as pleasant as possible for you. If you like they will also go out with you. But that's all! And if you should have needs, here are ten pesetas, and down the street there's a brothel. She said that to you in front of the whole family, in front of her daughters. They weren't in the least shocked, you say. It was possible to talk to the girls about anything, about the most intimate matters, at which every woman at home would turn red and say, please, you don't say things like that. Talk, just talk, that's all. That's how it was then in Castelserás.

In Sitges, twenty-five miles behind the front, you went to a brothel one evening out of pure curiosity. You drank a coffee and ate a piece of cake and talked to the girls, who wanted to know all kinds of things and were politically very smart, as you say, much smarter than the average. Then when they asked, what about it, comrade, are we going to the room, you declined, no, thanks, I'm tired, that's all, and they didn't press you any further, in this brothel in Sitges.

It was in the bend of the Ebro, just behind the front. A soldier tapped you on the shoulder, look, Sargento, there's a brothel over there. And he points to a small whitewashed clay barn. You walk over, there's a queue of soldiers. You pull open the door, or the gate, or there's no door at all any more on the rusty hinges, and you see some straw on the floor and four women, one in each corner, on top of each a man with his trousers down. At the door, you say, in front of the queue stood two men, civilians, they collected the money. You had them arrested, the two pimps and the four women, and sent the soldiers back to their posts. For a moment you puzzled over how they could have managed to cross the Ebro unchecked. That's all.

There were several volunteers who had Spanish girlfriends. It was a strange situation. We had contact with women, above all with the Barcelona women's organisation, which adopted us, so to speak. I can remember that once we were put in the frontline and then we were withdrawn, and that's when they visited us. But the girls weren't at all approachable. The women were perhaps approachable. For sex, I mean. With the girls, you could do anything, except sleep with them. It was a deep-seated attitude. After the war, in Paris, I was surprised that when I met Spanish women it was quite different. But earlier, you only had a chance with the girls if you promised to marry them. And there were a few Austrians who were prepared to marry the girls they had got to know. I can't remember specific cases. It wasn't so important to me. We were cautious, we took care not to be conspicuous in an immoral way, so we were reserved when it came to women, if they didn't take the initiative themselves. But as I said, there were a few who got involved in a steady relationship. And Friemel is even supposed to have married at the time. While he was still in Spain.

I know, I'll say to him, you would have liked to marry Marga on the spot. Because you loved her, really loved her. I can bear witness to that, even if it still hurts my old stupid heart to say so. You loved her, but you were afraid to tell her the truth. Because then my sister would not have been interested in you. Clear as day.

Because Rudi was already married, to an Austrian. And the Austrian had a child by him. A boy. That's clear as day too. But Rudi didn't come out with it until much later. He didn't talk much about himself at all. As talkative as he otherwise was, he became guarded when it came to his family. It was with good reason that one had to drag everything out of him. Because his father was a Nazi. He denounced his own wife, that's how it must have been, otherwise I don't understand how the woman ended up in a concentration camp. She was murdered there. Why, I don't know. I only know, that Rudi once told me, that she was killed.

That's utter nonsense. I can't imagine that my father told such lies.

Yes, that's what you said, Rudi. I heard you say so myself. Or did my sister tell me? Did I dream it?

The relationship between my father and my grandfather was always a very good one. The two did a lot together politically, and presumably, also privately. My grandmother tended to stay at home. I can't say whether my grandparents' marriage was a happy one. My feeling is that it wasn't, but I can't swear to it. She never came to political meetings. She died in 1936, while my father was in Wöllersdorf Detention Camp. From his letters it seems that she suffered from a serious illness. Perhaps cancer. At any rate, she died a natural death long before the Germans marched in, and my grandfather didn't denounce her either. From his curriculum vitae, which I found in the shoe box, it's absolutely clear that he never sympathised with the Right, whether Catholic or Nazi. He was always on the side of the Left. If it had been any different, I'm sure my mother would have mentioned it.

And that his sister killed herself. Rudi's sister. In the concentration camp. He said that too.

I don't remember my Aunt Steffi. All I know is that she once tried to commit suicide. She swallowed pills or turned on the gas, and my mother said, Steffi is a sly hussy, she knows exactly what to do, to make everyone feel sorry for her. But my aunt must have been serious about it, because in March '38 she threw herself out of the window, and there was no one there to stop her. There's a letter from my father, also in the shoe box, in which he tries to comfort my grandfather. Evidently he's very worried, because he begs my grandfather not to despair. And then he remembers a childhood experience, on an autumn day in 1916, when his mother was standing on Floridsdorf Bridge with Steffi and him and staring into the Danube below. 'She wanted finally to escape from our terrible need,' he writes. 'She wrestled with herself for a long, long time, weeping, she looked at the two of us again and again with an expression I'll never forget! And then she did go on fighting, until the whole rotten business was over. Father, you must not be any weaker than your wife was then; you have to struggle on, be just as tough as you have been up to now! For us there can be no flight from life.'

The two of them had a peculiarly close relationship, not like father and son, more like two brothers or like blood brothers who are forever true to one another.

At any rate Rudi was head over heels in love, and with Margarita, there's no getting away from that. I'm convinced, he would have liked nothing more than to marry her right there in Barcelona. But he was already married. Separated, but married. And his wife, the Austrian woman, didn't consent to a divorce.

Actually my mother never ever spoke ill of him. If she spoke ill of anyone, then of her father-in-law. As she saw it, he was to blame for my father getting involved with other women. But of her own accord she would never have pushed for a divorce. I remember, that a Herr Baburek, living in the same house, once said: Listen, what do you think you're doing? Why don't you get a divorce? I don't need to get a divorce, she replied, I'm not getting married again anyway.

She was bad, the Austrian woman. Rudi told me so himself. She even denounced him to the police. His own wife.

There's a letter, which my father wrote to her from Prague, after his flight, in April '34. In it he accuses her of having passed on some photographs to the police, as a result of which a number of his comrades were identified and arrested. He had furthermore heard, he writes, that she was refusing to let his parents into the flat and to let them see me. And that she was intending to have me baptised. He openly threatens her. 'It's not safe,' he writes, 'to oppose me. There were some who found out that wasn't good for their health. So think carefully about what you're doing!' Then he accuses her of having accepted money from the police welfare fund. He names a number of traitors and what happened to them because of their treachery. Dead, killed. Dead, shot. In hospital. Stabbed and badly beaten. He calls my mother: dirty slut.

I don't know what to think of this letter. I wish I had never read it.

Six months later Franco's troops entered Barcelona. With their terrible flag, with their terrible marches, with their terrible braying. The people were unrecognisable. They cheered like mad. They were probably afraid, perhaps they were simply glad that the war was over at last. The starvation and the poverty and the air raids every morning, every afternoon, every night. They clapped until their hands were sore. They were still clapping when Franco's legionaries, the Moors, were raping women. And when other women were offering themselves for a meal, for a pair of stockings or for the blessing of the Church. So prostitution and rapes and assault and arrests and executions without interruption. And still the clapping went on, the cheers of convinced republicans, Catalan nationalists, Socialists, rushing to open-air mass out of pure fear and enthusiasm.

My father had already died a couple of weeks earlier. He died almost from one day to the next. One night, during the blackout, he was knocked down by a cyclist. He got blood poisoning, it turned to gangrene, he perished wretchedly. In his final hours he asked for me, I had to bring his pipe to the hospital, just before nine in the evening, just as he always wanted it; I filled and lit it for him and put it between his teeth, he took one draw, smiled, coughed, then he died. My father was strong, he weighed almost twelve and a half stone. At the end he was well under eight stone.

Paco fled at four o'clock in the afternoon, when Franco's troops were already in the city. Marga and I had actually wanted to flee too. It was well-known that we were in Red Aid. At the hospital I had been promoted to lieutenant. So we had to get away. But my mother had a lot of silver, jewellery, lead crystal, she wanted to take it all with her.

I'm not going to leave it behind, am I, she said.

A coat and a blanket, you don't need any more than that, we said.

But she was unable to part with anything. So we ended up with a lot of baggage and there was no room for it on the truck.

You just go, she said, I'm staying here.

Out of the question.

So we stayed.

After the Fascists had occupied the city, she regretted not having fled.

I'm only in your way, she said, I'm making life difficult for you.

How are you making life difficult for us, what would we do without you?

But it was impossible to convince her that she wasn't a burden to us. Apart from that, she had got it into her head that she wanted to join my father.

We'll meet again in heaven, she said. It's God's will.

If that really is His will, I responded, why didn't He kill you together.

To which she replied: Because God lives in the next world.

And I: So, in the next world? And where in the next world, if I may ask? Where does He live, your God, in a villa or in a hut?

Oh Marina, don't say things like that. It's blasphemy.

But I couldn't be any different, I couldn't take her seriously. My mother was never a communist. She was a socialist, and a fairly limited one at that. She never understood the concept of free love, for example. Well, all right, she said. But the children belong to the mother. There was no convincing her otherwise. And now she was obsessed with killing herself. So that I go straight to heaven, where Francisco is waiting for me. To her my father was simultaneously her mother, her father, her uncle, her sister, her grandfather, her one and all. Without him she was nothing.

I kept my eye on her. At night I bound her to the bed, after she had twice got up to throw herself out of the window. Anyway, she managed to get round my sister: One night I hear noises, jump out of bed, switch on the light, there I see the two of them already standing on the balcony. I grab them, drag them back into the room, throw them both onto the bed.

It's true, my sister wanted to kill herself too, because her mother had convinced her: You're like me, Margarita, helpless and alone, what are you going to do in this world. Later on my sister tried to kill herself a couple of times. Despite her love for Rudi she didn't want to go on living. I'm not entirely blameless there, because in my despair the words slipped out, I didn't mean it like that. It happened on 1st May 1939, and it has ruined every 1st of May for me, even if, year after year, I take to the streets, demonstrate, ever since my father took me to a meeting as a small child.

On the 1st of May my mother was already in bed. She was still awake. Every evening I first took her into my bed, until she had calmed down, only then did I lead her to her room and bind her to the bed. But now she was still in my bed. And I absolutely had to go to the toilet. So I asked my sister to mind her. Be on your guard, I said, she mustn't move an inch. But hardly had I left the room than my mother began to flatter her: Margarita, you're good as gold, not nasty like Marina, be a dear, my sweet little girl, come, give me a kiss, I want to go to sleep. Leave me alone. And my stupid sister really is taken in. Yet it was only a couple of hours since my mother had tried to throw herself from the balcony.

So Margarita tucks her in, goes out of the room, and my mother immediately bolts the door. Margarita notices, rattles at the handle, I hear a muffled sound, an impact down in the street, run out of the toilet and shout: You've got her on your conscience, Margarita.

She never forgot that sentence. And that's why she tried to take her life in the nights that followed. Again and again she crept up to the window, I didn't shut my eyes once. For a whole week, night after night. Then a cousin took her in and slept in the same bed with her, Margarita on the side to the wall.

She was already very unstable as a child. My father never sent us to religious education, of course, but once she went to a children's holiday camp, and there the teachers drove her crazy with their fairy tales about Satan, about hellfire, about eternal damnation, it took her a long time to free herself of that, and something no doubt stuck.

In August a man I had known from before squealed on me. It was clear to me, we have to get away. And we set out for France, on foot, over the Pyrenees. First I sold everything, my mother's silver and my father's library and with the proceeds I paid a guide and bribed a policeman. Once we had crossed the border we went to an inn instead of buying two tickets for the bus. But we hadn't eaten anything for three days. I'll never forget the greasy face. The innkeeper's whiskery beard. He served us with extravagant courtesy. Just as we swallowed the last mouthful, there are two gendarmes standing beside us. Back to Spain or off to a camp! So we went to a camp. First to Saint-Cyprien. Then to Argelès. It was horrible there. Margarita was close to giving up. She grew weaker every day. Until a couple of women asked me to teach them reading and writing. They paid me with a pound of white bread, I slipped one piece to a little boy, the other to my sister. So we pulled through. In fact I played the part of the older sister all my life, although I was a year younger than Marga. But I was always the stronger one.

On 9th February we crossed the border at Port Bou. The Garde Mobile was waiting for us. We were part of a beaten army and representatives of a lost cause. The first we knew when we laid down our arms. The second only gradually dawned on us. In Saint-Cyprien, where we were simply trying to survive, we hardly had time to think. The camp was a long, narrow strip of land by the sea, surrounded by barbed wire. When we arrived there were no huts, no shelters, no toilets. We had to fight for every piece of bread and every mouthful of water. The French gloated over our suffering. They thought their officers who wanted to lure us into the Foreign Legion would have an easy job. But with very few exceptions we resisted being recruited. Today it's said that the Party leadership banned us from taking up the offer. It had interpreted the big war, which was imminent, as a conflict between the imperialist powers, which was no concern of ours. It may be, that at that point, that corresponded to Stalin's interests. But that wasn't the reason for our refusal; we would never have fought as mercenaries, not in our homelands, not in Spain, and we didn't want to do so now either. Quite coincidentally, apart from blind obedience to the Party we possessed something else which usually escapes the notice of historians and which today no one wants to grant us. In order to save this something, we wanted to stay together. Or find other possibilities of scraping a living outside the wire: emigration to England, Scandinavia, Mexico. I remember that Friemel put his name down on a list of Socialist veterans of the Spanish war who were requesting asylum in Sweden. I don't recollect that he mentioned his Spanish woman in that context. Nor did I know anything about their relationship. But that doesn't mean anything. Contrary to a commonly held belief, you hardly get to know others at times of great trouble. What good would it have done if he had written her name on the list? Was he even in touch with her? Did he know that she was about to flee to France as well? There were married couples among the Spanish republicans, imprisoned in Saint-Cyprien at the same time, men and women only separated by a six-foot fence, and who didn't find out until years later. We were ninety thousand people, herded together on a square kilometre. A medium-sized city, but without streets and houses, with an icy wind whistling down from the Pyrenees, fine sand that crunched between one's teeth.

We were in Saint-Cyprien from February to April '39. Then all the veterans of Spain were transferred to Gurs. Friemel was the representative of the Revolutionary Socialists in both Saint-Cyprien and Gurs. He was much liked, everyone thought highly of him, it was possible to discuss lots of things with him. Of course, he had his own line, his own ideas, that was normal, but he never took part in the campaign against us. Because there were some veterans, although hardly among the Austrians, who were absolutely demoralised and wanted to blame the Communists for everything. The camp administration stirred up the hate and the distrust. It got particularly bad after the German-Soviet Non-Aggression Pact. The French then regarded the Communists as murderers and gangsters and thieves and rogues and vagabonds, more or less. Naturally we had our differences too, the Pact, was it necessary, was it not necessary, betrayal, Stalin – we did discuss it, but not very intensively, which is also comprehensible. Because it was the Garde Mobile that was beating us up, not Hitler or Stalin.

In Gurs we set up an Adult High School on the Red Vienna model. We offered language courses, courses in literature, stenography, geography, history, mathematics; everyone who passed got a certificate. I don't know if Friemel got involved as well, most likely, almost everyone did. We weren't just concerned with further education; more important were a sense of solidarity and the need for distraction from events in the world outside and from the uncertainty about one's own future. Austria didn't exist any more, and the French got evident pleasure from reminding us of that. *Nationalité*, asked the officers, and when we answered:

Autrichien, they said: *Ah, un autre chien!*[1] After it hadn't worked with the Foreign Legion, they wanted to force us into their labour companies. At first we refused. But in time we had to give in. Then many of us reported for service, almost every second Austrian. We toiled away for the French everywhere from the Swiss border up to the Channel.

I don't know how Friemel managed to get out of Gurs. Perhaps he volunteered for duty. Perhaps he got permission, because he could prove his wife was waiting for him, things like that did happen. Or perhaps he was transferred to another camp, where women's visits were allowed. Or perhaps he simply cleared off, escaped over the fence at night or under the fence. Anyway, one day he was gone.

Then our camp was wound up. Everyone able to work must work! I was taken, because I was strong, but not my sister, she was too delicate and frail.

If she's not allowed to work, then I'm not going either.

Well, all right, they said.

The French put us on cattle trucks, I'll never forget that, forty women in each truck. We were unloaded in Savoie, not far from the Swiss border. We were supposed to work as farm-girls there. I was assigned to a countess, she lived in a real castle, and next to the castle were the farm buildings, with stable, sheds and barn. Marga ended up with a woman who farmed in Sillingy, a village about twenty miles away. There at least she had enough to eat. I don't know how Rudi managed to find her. In any case, one day

1. An untranslatable pun on *autrichien* (Austrian) and *autre chien* (another dog) – (translator)

33

he visited her. By then he was no longer locked up, he could move about freely. Somehow they ran into each other's arms. Then Margarita was pregnant.

Once my employment contract was up, I went to fetch her. Her employer wanted to keep me there. I've always been rebellious, stubborn, never let anyone get the better of me. Marga, on the other hand, was the typical little woman. She liked to dress well, put on make-up, lipstick. But she was squeamish. She just would not want to muck out the stalls, milk or pick potatoes. And the farmer was fed up to the back teeth with her. A pity, she said, when she saw me. If I'd only had one like you! And I really did get stuck in, there in the country. The first time I was supposed to drive the cattle onto the meadow, all fourteen broke away, down the street at full gallop, into the church. The whole village had to help to get them out again. By which I mean to say that my work was no picnic.

From Annecy we took the train to Montauban. Right across France for two days, without papers! The Gestapo was already everywhere. The Germans. My sister was shaking with fear. Before each check I sent her to the toilet. Bolt the door, I told her, and don't open up until I tell you. Then when the Germans came I put on my brightest smile. Excusez-moi, monsieur. Unfortunately my sister has taken the documents with her. She's just gone to the smallest room. If you would like to wait... It worked every time. Only once did one of these squareheads rattle the toilet door. Open up, control! I rushed out of my compartment, I pounced on him like a fury: Take your paws off the door handle! My sister has been vomiting. She's expecting a child. The German stared at me, then he disappeared into the next carriage. Lucky for him! Otherwise I would have scratched his eyes out.

We arrived in Montauban on 2nd October, on my twenty-third birthday. We took a furnished room. Marga wrote to Rudi. By that time he was a miner, a face-worker in the coal mines at Carmaux. He came to fetch her on the third day. Then I heard nothing more from them. Until my sister gave birth, on 26th April 1941. I visited them then. I immediately fell in love with my little nephew. Rudi came after a while. We embraced. Then I already had to travel back.

Margarita gave birth in Albi, in a maternity hospital, like me. Neither of us was lucky. Because she was kicked, so that the boy finally came out, and me they almost had to cut open, they pulled my boy out with forceps. There are easy births, but we suffered for ever. My contractions lasted three days, hers lasted two. So one says to oneself, if the birth is already so bad, then one should at least give the child a good life. Do everything, so as not to lose it. But Rudi didn't understand that. He lost his boy. He was only with him in the first few weeks and then the one night they were allowed to spend together. Apart from that he never saw him.

The question of repatriation became urgent with the armistice between France and Germany. After the German army had overrun the French positions, the country was divided in two. The camps were in the south, in the free zone, which was not so free at all. One day we had to fall in, and there were German officers there who called on us to return home. You have nothing to fear, they said, you are from the Ostmark, you haven't broken German laws, the Reich needs every national comrade! You will, however, be re-educated at home. They didn't tell us what that meant. So what about it, who's coming forward? In Le Vernet, where I was at the time, only one man volunteered. All the rest said, no, we're staying.

Then the Party did a U-turn. Perhaps it hoped that because of the German-Soviet Pact, the Nazis wouldn't harm the Communists. At any rate the instruction came from outside, the cadres had to be saved, everyone was falling apart in France, there was no perspective. We should consider volunteering sooner or later. To go home. It wasn't so unreasonable. Czech and Yugoslav veterans of the war had already volunteered for labour service in Germany. Hundreds of them had left. And they had actually found work. We knew that, because we got letters from them. They wrote to us that they were working in one factory or another and that things were better than in these bloody camps in France.

I visited them again two weeks later. To give my sister a hand with her little boy. That's when Rudi told me that he intended returning to Austria and taking Marga and little Edi with him. What an idea! My brother-in-law had fled Austria. He had got into trouble with the Nazis. He had fought against the Fascists in Spain. And this man wants to voluntarily give himself up to the Germans. I was dumbfounded.

Have you gone out of your mind! Do you absolutely want to die! If you must, then go back secretly, disguised as a foreign worker, with forged papers. But not officially!

We argued like mad. I said, what on earth put it into your head to take your wife, and your newborn child with you. Do you want them to kill all of you? And he, furious: Margarita, you can choose. Either your sister or me. Good, I said, I'll take my sister with me right now. But of course she decided to stay with him. She was head over heels in love with him. He was the father of her child. I wanted to throttle him. Throttle him or kiss him.

Please stay, I would have said.

There was no point in staying any longer. So we got used to the idea of going home. However, the Party issued the following instruction: No one who is subject to the Nürnberg race laws should go. But one of us, who as a half-Jew was affected by these laws, volunteered nevertheless. A well-known functionary, I won't mention his name, because he's dead, and one shouldn't speak ill of the dead. We expelled him at any rate, because he disregarded a Party decision. So no one subject to the Nürnberg Laws should go, and no one on whom the Nazis wanted to take revenge. We had one veteran of the Spanish war, for example, who had been involved in a gunfight with them, in the Hausruck district of Vienna, there had even been a couple of dead. He didn't volunteer either. That's how it was. And all the rest had to make up their own minds, whether they wanted to stay in France or report for the return transport. But there was no unequivocal order. It was left up to each individual, whether he wanted to travel home or not. But I would like to emphasise that the overwhelming majority decided, yes, I'm going. Not all. Yes, I'm going. Then we wrote to the German Armistice Commission in Toulouse and requested repatriation to Germany. Each man individually. Or not. Some didn't write.

Even today I don't understand why he went back to Germany. I can't get it into my head. He wasn't the only one, there were many who volunteered, one of them was called Hans. Hans was very attractive, a giant of a man, well over six foot. He wanted to take me to the registry office, and from the registry office straight

to Germany. I said: Not me. Even if you bound me hand and foot
I wouldn't come. Although I did go back too, to Spain, to the
dictatorship, voluntarily. I too came back here with my son. I said
to myself, if they shoot me – then let them shoot me. But they
won't get my boy, Julián will make it somehow. Just let the
Fascists shoot me. The only reason they didn't shoot me is that I
wasn't sentenced until 1945. Germany was already defeated by
then, and Franco was shit-scared of the Allies. The court nevertheless wanted to impose the maximum sentence. What I mean
to say is, that I went voluntarily too, but wild horses wouldn't
have got me to Germany. OK, if the Fascists can't prove anything
against a person. But someone like Rudi, with his Red past, on
the run, a wanted man, who had fled Vienna... no, no and no
again. I've no idea if his son knows, I've never said a word to him
at least. I was convinced the man had cracked up.

Of course, there was a lot of discussion about it. And there were
weighty arguments against. First, it's a journey into the unknown.
Second, you can never trust a Nazi, he promises everything possible and never keeps his word. Third, you'll end up in a concentration camp or imprisoned somewhere else. Such considerations
were on everyone's mind: Do I have to take the risk? Yes or no.
But there was also the hope: Perhaps we'll get work, like the
Yugoslavs. And anyway, what's going to happen to us in France?
Are we going to survive or starve? Or go underground? That
wasn't a solution either, or only for a very few. Because the
Germans would have tracked us down everywhere, and if not
them, then the French collaborating with them. Anyone who
didn't volunteer, the Gestapo got hold of them one way or
another.

I don't mean to say that I didn't understand his decision. Many returned secretly, to Spain or to Germany or to Austria, which at that time didn't exist. I understood very well why they did it. I would also have understood if he had gone secretly to Germany, armed, to fight in the resistance. That's the way we thought then. We risked our lives, our happiness, our health, everything for freedom. I took the risk. I have never regretted it. But I wasn't as naive as Rudi. Signs up officially, together with his wife and child.

Friemel made the request. I'm certain that he did his best to play down his own role in the fight against National Socialism, like every one of us. For example, we emphasised our opposition to the Dollfuss regime, which the Nazis also hated, and that we went to Spain, because we couldn't get any work in Austria. Friemel will also have written that he avoided transport back for so long because he didn't want to leave his wife behind alone. And that he hopes to find work in Germany in the trade he had learned. But he will not have lied. He will not have forced a declaration of loyalty to the German Reich out of himself. He will have made the request on 1st June 1941.

A letter from the Repatriation Commissioner of the German Armistice Commission in Toulouse will have reached him one week later: To 'Herr Rudolf Friemel 9 Place de l'Eglise Arthès (Tarn). I have today made arrangements with the French authorities for you to be handed over to the German authorities at the line of demarcation. The transfer will be carried out by French gendarmerie officers in plain clothes. Also enclosed is 1 repatriation pass, which is accepted by all relevant authorities as confirmation that you are a Reich or Volks German and that you are being repatriated by me as Repatriation Commissioner of the German Armistice Commission. This pass does not, however, entitle you to leave your present place of residence without authorisation or to independently cross the line of demarcation. I request you to remove the section attached to the transfer document, affix your signature and the transfer date and send it to me immediately using the stamped addressed envelope included. It is essential that you do this.

Lutz. German Red Cross Field Officer.'

Friemel will have complied with the instructions.

Rudi defended his decision. I have to fight, he said. I said, how are you going to fight, when they're just waiting for you. You're running straight into their arms.

And even if I am, I have to help liberate my country.

At that I became angry. If you must run headlong into disaster, then do it alone. Do what you must. It's your life. But leave the boy and my sister here. And he: It's my family. They belong to me. I don't have anyone else. I'll take care of them.

They're staying here!

They're coming with me!

And then he says: Margarita, you have to decide. Either your sister or me.

That's how it was. He threw me out. Of course, I undermined his arguments. Margarita was wavering. He realised that, and so he became angry. Later my sister once told me, you were right Marina, I should have gone with you.

He was obsessed by the desire to free Austria from fascism. Good, I see that. But then why didn't he go back alone, to test the water? If nothing had happened to him, he could have let Margarita follow later. Then perhaps many things wouldn't have happened. It was your fault, Rudi, for all that you mean to me. You were crazy. If one has a child, then one has to think carefully before every step. A child comes first, I think. And that's what I told them: Have you gone out of your minds, the boy is only three months old. I was close to grabbing him by the throat, just to save Marga and the child. Even though I liked Rudi, more than liked him. But I was in a rage, because of the boy, because of the boy above all. Because my sister was young, healthy, strong, but little Edi? The poor mite. Only just born.

You were also asked: What does Rudi say about it? He must have made up his mind. What does the Party want? Has it really decided that we should go back? And you expressed your personal opinion: It's more sensible to go to Germany than to go to the dogs in France. Of course it's dangerous and a leap in the dark, but at least we're out of this shit, it won't be so bad, and your country is your country. Let's go home! As simple as that.

We made up again when we said goodbye. Rudi embraced me. I kissed little Edi, then my sister. They had a compartment to themselves. They put the boy in the luggage rack. As the train left, they leaned out of the window, laughing, as if the happy ending was just around the corner.

It was a muggy July morning, July '41. There was a thunderstorm in the afternoon.

2

THE PROOF

All the dead rest in the restlessness of a perhaps unnecessary death. You know the sentence. It often goes through my head. I regret nothing, or very little. I admit, however, I was too impetuous. It's not as if I believed I could outrun time. I already knew then, it's futile, it always catches up. Nor did I believe that love would save me. Love and time either like one another or are deadly enemies, one cannot exist without the other. I fervently believed in the times, in my bearing witness to the times, just as I fervently believed in our love. Why should I have doubted it? But time is always stronger than love. That, too, is a sentence, which in the restlessness of my perhaps unnecessary death, I do not want to accept. Look at me. I'm smiling. I'm wearing thin striped prisoner's trousers. I'm wearing a wedding shirt embroidered with roses. Time like love. There's nothing more to be seen.

A wedding, in Auschwitz? Between a prisoner and a woman from outside? With a bouquet for the bride and a wedding march? Who told you that fairy tale?

– I heard about it, years later. No, didn't hear, read it. Don't remember where now.

– The Nazis would never have allowed anything like that. And if they did, then only as a joke. To have fun at the expense of the poor devils. The way the escapees they had caught were brought back on a cart with a placard around their necks: 'Here I am again!' and the prisoners' orchestra had to strike up: 'Kommt ein Vögel geflogen… ' ('Comes a bird a-flying…')

– Why not? In hell everything is possible, even heaven.

– Impossible. There was a registry office in the camp, but it was only concerned with registering the dead.

– Each registry office had three functions: Record of births, record of marriages, record of deaths.

– I cannot imagine that a regular marriage ceremony would have been permitted. Except to allay suspicions, so that the Nazis could boast: See, how well our prisoners are being looked after. The rumours about mass extermination – just atrocity propaganda put out by our enemies. But in '44 no one was interested in the effect of such an event any more – by that time the murderers had long before come to terms with their bad reputation, the collaborators with their bad conscience and the opponents with their powerlessness.

– Wait a minute! The propaganda film about Theresienstadt was not made until 1944, autumn '44. So why no wedding in Auschwitz.

– Höss was removed as camp commandant in November '43. His successor, Liebehenschel, made an effort to reduce the terror. He broke the supremacy of the criminal kapos. For the first time a man with a red triangle, that is, a political prisoner, became camp elder. Liebehenschel issued a bunker amnesty. He ordered the standing cells and the Black Wall to be demolished. He got rid of the death sentence. He prohibited beating during interrogation. He also took action against the intimidation through informers encouraged by the Political Section. Presumably it is thanks to him that the marriage ceremony was permitted. No?

– The father of the bridegroom is supposed to have had good connections in Berlin, all the way up to Himmler. No?

– The bride was Spanish. So it's conceivable that Franco, as an ally of Hitler, supported the wedding. Not that either?

– The SS men were gradually beginning to realise that the war was lost. Some of them became bloody friendly. They began to collect bonus points. The wedding was a big bonus point. Or not?

– We should not assume that the Nazis acted logically. Logical thinking was alien to them. Decisions about life and death were completely arbitrary. For example, I was sentenced for actions preparatory to committing high treason, but not executed. But at the same time others were immediately guillotined for quite trivial offences. It was no different in the camp. Nine hundred and ninety-nine were killed, the thousandth got away with it. We shouldn't try to see a purpose behind every permission and behind every exceptional permission and behind every fart of a Nazi. The wedding took place, that much is certain.

The only thing that's certain is that immediately after their arrival in Vierzon, while they were still on the platform, they were separated. The Secret Military Police detained him, and Marga was forced to travel on to Germany with Edi. Perhaps the men allowed them to take leave of each other. I don't think it was a tearful farewell. Tears need time, and they only had thirty seconds.

Apart from that he was hoping to see her again soon. It didn't even occur to him that the story, hardly begun, could have an unhappy ending. It is also not the case that the men shouted at them or even hit them. Probably they were even polite. Nevertheless, Marga was very frightened. Where are they taking you, Rudi, she may have said. What is to become of us. Why are they separating us. How will we manage without you. Don't be afraid, he will have replied. Take good care of Edi. And never forget to say that we're married. That's important! Don't be sad, it'll only be a couple of days. I love you.

I love you too.

She saw him for the last time as he walked across the tracks between the German policemen. He turned round and raised his arm. She waved back. Then she turned a little to the side, so that he could also see Edi, whom she was clasping to her breast, just one more time.

That was on 31st July 1941. Two weeks later Rudi was taken to Dijon Prison. He wrote that in his notebook: Arrival Dijon, 15 Aug., 4.30 pm. But what had happened to him in the meantime, and what happened afterwards?

It is quite possible that he was transferred to Bourges the very same evening or the following day. He would have been locked up there for two weeks, in the prison or in a barracks with other veterans of the Spanish War. Because he also made this entry in his notebook: Departure Bourges, 12 Aug., 12 noon. The young recruits who were detailed to guard duty would have treated him correctly and furtively quizzed him about his experiences in Spain. Only a sergeant will have bawled him out, made him stand to attention and called him a Jewish lackey, Bolshevist, Communard. But his bark is worse than his bite, he will have thought. Once he would have inquired about Marga. The Wehrmacht is not responsible for family matters, he would have been told. Who is? The Foreign Organisation of the Party. Where? In Paris. This entry too is to be found in his notebook: 7 Aug. 41. For. Org. of the NSDAP: Paris, 15 rue Beaujon. Gradually the cells will have filled with other returnees, also with thieves, black marketeers, Foreign Legionaries who had been picked up, men accused of undermining morale, deserters, others who had refused to obey orders. One morning they would have been marched to the railway station and on a siding, cordoned off from civilians, herded onto a waggon. Rudi would have been lucky because he would have been one of the first to climb onto the goods waggon, so he would have been able to secure a place beside a grille, with a view of an occupied country. The men of the escort would have sat further to the front in a partitioned area, played cards and drunk wine. They would have made only slow progress, would have halted repeatedly, once the truck would even have been uncoupled, and they would have had to wait a whole day in a shunting yard, in the heat and stench, without permission to empty the bucket in which they relieved themselves. Only after three days would they have reached Dijon. And from Dijon, by way of several intermediate stops in German prisons, he would have been brought to Vienna.

Or maybe not.

Because it is also conceivable that the military police only held him in Dijon for one night and already the next morning transferred him to Paris, to the Santé. Perhaps he even ended up in Cell 23, the same cell in which I had frozen and starved six months earlier. Once a day, for him as for me, the warder pushed a bowl through the just-open door, filled with three-tenths of a litre of water, in which a wrinkled carrot and half a potato were floating. I don't know how he coped with the hunger, being alone and the worry about his wife and child. Perhaps he suddenly broke out in a hot sweat, because in the rush he had forgotten to write down his father's address for Marga. It's possible that then he jumped up and pounded the door with his fists. But even before the warder came to see what was up he had recovered his composure. He asked to be allowed a book to read. The next day the man threw a tattered copy of Schiller's *William Tell* into his cell, as he had thrown it in for me. Days later, he banged on the door again, work, make myself useful, and truly a little old man in a blue suit appeared, a roll of wire in his hand, and showed him, as he showed me, how to make a rat trap. He set to work immediately and in three days had made forty traps. As a reward, the old man slipped him, as he slipped me, a little packet of tobacco, papers and matches. I smoked it all, but he kept one cigarette paper, in order to write a poem on it, in tiny letters, in Spanish for his Spanish wife, and he called the poem 'Mi dulce mujer'.

Even as he was still writing, he heard the shout outside in the corridor: Vingt-trois! and the warder unlocked the door and led him to a room, in which two Gestapo men were waiting. Then a woman was dragged in as well, pale and hunched up, with a hunted look. In the prison yard they were pushed into a taxi and taken for interrogation through deserted streets, to Avenue Foch. During the journey one of the guards said to the woman: I hope you're going to be more talkative this time, and at these words the woman started. And the man said to him, as he said to me: Well, unless you're a good boy, you're going to get a good hiding now. You won't know what's hit you.

Despite the threat the interrogation passed off better than

expected. First of all the Gestapo officers held out the prospect of better rations. One of them even gave him a sandwich during a break. He waited for the first blow nevertheless, and he tensed his muscles, so as not to fall to his knees right away. But the blows didn't come, even when he, like me, answered their questions evasively. He realised that they knew a bit about him, but not that in Spain he had been a political delegate, and he very wisely didn't mention that. Basically they were only interested in those former comrades from the Social Democratic Schutzbund, who had emigrated to the Soviet Union in 1934 and from there had gone to fight in the Spanish Civil War. They read out names to him, as they did to me, Tränkler, Tesar, Barak, Beyer, Distelberger... and like me he shook his head each time, don't know him, don't know him either, never heard of him, or nodded when it came to those he couldn't harm any more, because they had fallen near Madrid or at Teruel or during the Ebro offensive or because they had volunteered for the Foreign Legion in Saint-Cyprien. Don't forget, he said, that most of the volunteers in Spain adopted false names. They were satisfied with this information. Or not. If they weren't, then they slapped him, whipped him, knocked him to the ground, pulled him up by the hair, poured cold water over him. He said nothing.

I don't know if she was a help to him. I don't know if he remained silent, because he knew that she loves him. I only know: Arrived Dijon, 15 Aug. Arrived Vienna, 14 Nov. Did they transfer him to Compiègne? Dijon was the collecting point for all the deportees of the area, before they were taken to Compiègne. Later the author Jorge Semprún wrote about it. He described how, before being transported from Dijon to Compiègne, he or the character in his novel was shackled to an old man, a Pole, who spoke broken French and constantly whispered only one sentence: This is it, now they're going to kill us all. Semprún or his hero, at any rate a Spaniard called Manuel or Gérard, had tried to calm down the Pole, don't worry, comrade, no one wants to kill us. During the night the train came to a halt in the middle of nowhere, and then the man beside him had wheezed: Can you hear? He had heard nothing, only the breathing of their fellow prisoners. What, he had whispered. The screams. What screams. The screams of those being massacred, there, beneath the train. He had said nothing, because it had been pointless to calm down the other, who after a couple of seconds began to talk again: The blood, don't you hear the blood flowing. Under the train, there, rivers of blood, I can hear them flowing. Be quiet, you bastard! A German soldier had shouted and struck the Pole in the chest with his rifle butt, so violently, that the man, as he was vomiting blood and phlegm, had fallen forward and, since they were handcuffed together, pulled Manuel-Gérard down with him. Was Rudi there, in the train from Dijon to Compiègne, at night, together with the Pole and with Manuel-Gérard, Marga's fellow countryman?

He was never transferred to Compiègne. Instead he was taken home with his countrymen, from France by way of Trier, Regensburg, Nürnberg, Würzburg to Vienna. Or to Vienna by way of Karlsruhe, Bruchsal and Linz. Perhaps like me he was locked up in a prisoner transport waggon at Karlsruhe Station, in a narrow cell with a small opening in the wall between it and the next cell, and, like me, he communicated through the crack with a German criminal, who instead of a left hand had an iron hook, like a pirate. The man told him, as he told me, that he had chopped off his hand himself. The Nazis, he whispered, had sent him to a fen camp, where the prisoners had to cut peat or remove the peat with a wheelbarrow, and any peat-cutter who didn't manage the required daily quota was beaten half to death, and so he chopped the hand off – and he wasn't the only one: There were many who chopped off their hands, and after they recovered they got an iron hook screwed on to the stump and were then overjoyed, and he too was overjoyed because with an iron hook he was only capable of pushing a wheelbarrow, and pushing a wheelbarrow was pure pleasure compared to cutting peat.

Friemel didn't allow himself to be scared by these remarks. He thought, perhaps the man is lying, perhaps he lost the hand in an accident at work and anyway – we, the veterans of the Spanish war, aren't criminals like the man with the hook. We'll be treated better. And he was treated better, in Vienna, in the police jail on Elisabeth Promenade, which he was already familiar with, from 1934 or '35, when he was awaiting trial there.

I don't know who was in charge of his case at Gestapo headquarters on Morzinplatz. Perhaps it was the former detective inspector who had trailed Rudi in 1934, during Austro-Fascism, and who had gone over to the Nazis in good time. The shared past of hunter and hunted aroused in the man a complicated feeling of brotherhood in arms; it could have been like that, it would explain why, only a few days after his arrival, Rudi got permission to write a card to his father. There was a certain amount of competition between the Gestapo people and the prison officers in the Lizzy as we almost affectionately called the prison. They were envious of each other's prisoners. An example: When I was being brought back to the Lizzy from Morzinplatz by a

Gestapo officer, the man indicated to me that I should stop outside a tobacconist's. He put a ration coupon in my hand. Buy a packet of 'Sport', he said, and when I came out the door again: Don't let the Käs take them off you. Käs, that was the Austrian term for trusty. Rudi will have taken advantage of the mutual distrust between Gestapo and police warders. It's also possible that he saw old acquaintances in the Lizzy again – one or two retired warders, who had to return to duty now, because the younger ones had been called up. Because in the Lizzy too Rudi got privileged treatment. On his first card he already writes to his father that he is a domestic worker. An important position. Domestic workers didn't have to stay in their cells during the day, they didn't starve, because when food was doled out, there was always a helping left over for them, they could smuggle cigarettes, read newspapers and pass on secret messages. Not all domestic workers behaved decently. I remember one prisoner who, like the criminals, demanded a mark for a cigarette. A veteran of the Spanish war, but an arsehole, unlike Rudi.

He wrote his last letter to my mother in July '39, when he was still being held in the camp at Gurs. It's a cool, controlled letter, in which as if through clenched teeth he asks her for divorce by mutual agreement. He justifies his request by saying the marriage only exists on paper anyway, that under no circumstances will he deviate from his path and that given the situation it's inconceivable that he will return home. He will not, of course, evade his material responsibilities; should she have misgivings in this respect, then he will give her the possibility of initiating the separation because of fault on his side. The matter is urgent, he writes, because only as an unmarried man does he have any chance of getting away to Mexico or Argentina, and so having any prospect of work and earnings. He didn't give her any further reason. Somehow she then found out that he had formed a liaison with another woman. She never talked about it. I assume it hurt her.

In his letter my father also declares that he had never forgotten me. He loves me, he writes, more than ever. He would so like to have me with him, to show me his life, which is not so bad, as she perhaps thinks. He hopes that she is bringing me up to be a person of whom his father needs to be as little ashamed as his mother. 'And if later on I should no longer be alive, then tell him, that his father always thought of him, that he would have liked to stay with his son, if he had been able to; grandfather should then tell him about the side of my life which you never knew and could not know.'

At his request my mother then filed for divorce by mutual agreement. She thereby gave up the right to maintenance. I'm surprised that she accepted the letter at all. The post normally came via my grandfather, he then sent it to my mother, and my mother often sent it back. She didn't even open the envelopes. Among my grandfather's things I've found the note: 'Last letter to Paula was not accepted.'

At any rate they were divorced. The divorce certificate was issued by the Vienna District Court on 16th August 1941. So in that respect at least my father was a free man when he was committed to the police prison on 14th September.

When he was locked up there, I already had Dachau behind me. They put him in Cell 78a, which was on the fourth floor, and a couple of weeks before they had taken me out of 44a, on the second floor. I assume that his cell was more or less identical to mine: fairly big, a room really, with four or six plank beds and at least a dozen prisoners. In a corner, completely exposed, the loo. Those who didn't have a bed slept on mattresses, which were piled up in a corner during the day. We were quite a mixed crowd, all political prisoners at the disposal of the Gestapo: five or six veterans of Spain, a factory worker who had broken his ankle while skiing at Easter and on being admitted to hospital was arrested for forming Communist cells, a con man, who had posed as an SS captain up on the Semmering, although he was a member neither of the SA or the SS, a so-called economic offender, whose crime I no longer remember, a Serbian diplomat, who had been arrested after Hitler's attack on Yugoslavia, a French tramp, who for obscure reasons had chosen Nazi Germany as his destination, a retired colonel who had been reported by his home help for listening to enemy broadcasting stations, and an Austrian communist of Jewish origin, whom the Soviet secret police had handed over to the Gestapo. His name was Franz Koritschoner, he was not yet fifty, but looked like an old man. Whereas the other Spanish veterans kept their distance from him as if he was a leper, I arranged things so that we were lying next to one another in the evening; so that's how I learned about Koritschoner's experiences in the Soviet Union, where he had spent several years in various camps on the Arctic Ocean as a supposed Nazi spy or Trotskyite – which was the same thing to us at the time. He had fallen ill with scurvy, as a result of which all his teeth had fallen out. Despite his fate he was not bitter. He firmly believed that the wrong turn in the Soviet Union – that's what he called it: a wrong turn – would be corrected. As far as his own future was concerned, he was cautiously optimistic. Things could hardly be worse in the German concentration camps than on the Pechora

River and in Vorkuta. The Gestapo had informed his sister that he was being transferred to Mauthausen. But as I found out after the war, Koritschoner finally ended up in Auschwitz. One day after his arrival, on 8th June 1941, he was registered as deceased. So Rudi didn't come across him, in one place or the other.

Rudi's cell was, I imagine, occupied by similar people, comrades from Spain, who didn't lose courage even now, resistance fighters prepared for the worst and who were in need of our inadequate comfort, crooks who in those great times had been tempted into small jobs, which cost them their heads. Only someone like Koritschoner will not have been in Cell 78a, and I don't know if his presence would have had a favourable or unfavourable effect on Rudi's state of mind or none at all.

I can't say whether Rudi was already reckoning on Auschwitz then. Presumably he hoped to be transferred to Mauthausen. Stupid as we were, and confident in our patriotism, we all longed for Mauthausen. We didn't have a clue about the death quarry, about the death stairs, about the death tunnels. He knew at any rate that a concentration camp lay in store, because in his card of 24th September, he wrote to his father that he would probably only be in the Lizzy for a few weeks. He asked for tomatoes, green peppers, some fruit, also for a small tube of toothpaste, an old nightshirt and a couple of shoe insoles. He instructed his father to go at 2 pm on a Tuesday to the officer handling his case at Gestapo headquarters at 4 Morzinplatz, Room 274. He asked him to take away the dirty laundry (likewise on a Tuesday, between 5.30 and 6 pm). Most important, however, and even the deliberately cheerful tone betrays it, appears to be his request to find out the address of Margarita Friemel-Ferrer from the

Foreign Organisation of the NSDAP in Paris. 'Is it a surprise to you?' he writes. 'Doesn't matter! Give my address to the "For. Org." with the request to forward it to Margarita. Enclose return postage.' I assume that his father, who was practised in such things, was immediately able to obtain permission to visit. As a rule, meetings between Gestapo prisoners and their relatives took place in what was called the closed section, on the ground floor of the prison building, to the left after the entrance and always in the presence of a warder and a Gestapo man. A concertina barrier separated the prisoners from their visitors. Visiting time was limited to three minutes. An open conversation was impossible under such conditions. In Rudi Friemel's case, however, I think it possible that he was able to talk to his father for much longer than the allotted time. Or that it was possible for them to exchange news via a resolute prison warder, who acted as courier. Rudi's second card to his father, of 10th November, at any rate suggests comprehensive discussion of his situation. Clemens Friemel had evidently been requested by Paris to provide further information in order to trace Frau Margarita Friemel-Ferrer, because Rudi writes, he hopes his father has already received and forwarded the required details. 'You don't know what an enormous weight you would take from me, if you would succeed in finding out Marga's place of residence.' In addition he refers to 'the petition we discussed', which he had handed in, but to which he 'had so far received no reply of any kind'. 'Will also apply for permission to be allowed to remain here in Vienna as long as possible, if the petition should be rejected.' None of us in Gestapo custody lodged any kind of petition. And it wouldn't have been approved anyway. So I suspect that from the very first Rudi fought to be able to marry the Spanish woman with such energy, that he was even able to impress the Gestapo people. Because the petition cannot have been about anything else, but the request to marry. That no decision was made is another matter.

They put a document like that in front of every one of us. It always had the same letterhead, the same signature, the same principal clause: Reich Security Headquarters Berlin SW 11, Prinz Albrecht Strasse 8. Signed Heydrich. 'Grounds for the preventive detention order: According to the observations of the State Police he endangers the continued existence and security of the nation by his behaviour...' The nice distinction lay in the formulation of the subordinate clause, but even for that the desk brains in Berlin had only four or five variations up their sleeves. The variant intended for him, as for me, read: '...in that he was to a considerable extent involved in Marxist activities and participated in the Civil War in Spain on the side of the Reds, so there is reason to fear, should he be released, that he may exploit the war situation to carry out activities harmful to the Reich.'

His preventive detention order was already made out on 11th October 1941. He signed it on 12th December at 3 pm, in the group cell on the ground floor of the prison building, to which we were transferred shortly before departure. That would mean that he was put on a transport on 13th December, at latest on the 16th. He was therefore in transit for a long time and with many detours. The Russian campaign was in full swing, the railway lines going east were overburdened. All wheels are rolling for victory, was the watchword. Rudi wasn't winning any victories, on the way he had to wait again and again. Because we know that he didn't arrive in Auschwitz on a group transport until 2nd January 1942. The eighteen prisoners were given the numbers 25167 to 25184. Rudolf Friemel was number 25173.

I returned to Spain at the beginning of October 1941. In Montauban the Gestapo was close on my heels. My brother was in the Resistance, and his group was being supplied with money and leaflets through me. The Germans soon became suspicious. They interrogated me in the maternity hospital the first time. I had given birth at five am, and at eight they were standing by my bed. Four weeks later they turned my room upside down, but only found receipts of nine money transfers.

And what about this, they asked.

Oh, nothing, I said, they're just maintenance payments.

What, from nine different men? You're not trying to tell us that you've been carrying on a relationship with all of them.

Certainly, I said.

They wanted to have it in writing. So I confirmed that I was the concubine of all nine. Two days later I cleared off. I knew, if I wait any longer, they'll get me.

In fact, there were two reasons to go over the border. First of all, the Spanish Party had issued the instruction, everyone who is able to take the risk should return. To me they presented it as if there was nothing to think about. And I didn't think for long. If they had said, at the stroke of midnight you have to stand at the Cibeles Fountain in Madrid in spotted underpants, then I would have turned up in the spotted underpants. That's how it was then. Apart from that I wanted my boy to be in good hands. Julián was just one month old. And with the Gestapo breathing down my neck I simply couldn't take the risk of remaining in France. I wasn't even keen to have a child. It was Fernando's fault. He wasn't careful. Once the boy was there, I was happy, of course, but to begin with... I knew the situation we were in. At any rate, it was immediately clear to me: From this moment I bear responsibility for a child, who is not to blame for the involvements and struggles of his parents. That's exactly what I reproach Rudi with: that he didn't think of the child. I made sure that my boy is protected, that there is someone to look after him, if they should catch me. And they did catch me.

I set out on 1st October. On the second I was in Perpignan, to say goodbye to Fernando, and so that he could at last take his child in his arms, and on the fourth I crossed the border at Port Bou. I had hardly set foot on Spanish soil than I was met by a crowd of nuns and a squad of Guardia Civil. In those days Spain was overrun with nuns and Guardias, they settled like swarms of locusts and stripped the land bare. The police questioned me immediately. But it didn't do them any good. I told them nothing but lies. I don't think I've ever lied so well as under Franco. Not a word about having spent the Civil War years in Barcelona. I was an auxiliary nurse, I said, in a hospital in Madrid. But I had only lived in Madrid until I was sixteen. Of course, they didn't find anything about me in their files. So they let me go. And I went to Minorca, where there were uncles and aunts of mine, my father's brothers and sisters. They were rolling in money. All the better for my boy, I said to myself. I could look after him properly, there was milk, there was bread, there were vegetables, there was even a warm bed. I stayed in Minorca until the boy was seven months old. Then I went to Madrid with him. My husband's parents naturally wanted to see their grandchild. Apart from that Fernando had now also returned to Spain, with a disabled transport. They let him in, even though at the border he could think of nothing better to do than to bellow the Marseillaise at the top of his voice. The French gendarmes stood to attention when they heard him singing, but a Falangist in the next carriage wanted to have him arrested right away as a provocateur.

I hadn't heard a thing from Rudi and Margarita since their departure. It wasn't until much later that I found out that my sister had ended up in a village somewhere in the Black Forest. There she was on her feet for fourteen or sixteen hours a day, as dogsbody in a butcher's, and little Edi was put in a nursery. She was only allowed to see him once a week. Because of her black hair she was taken to be a Jew and there was hostility towards her because of that, the woman in charge of the home bossed her around, she was too slow for the butcher's wife, she had no word from Rudi. She was quite desperate, and that's why she wrote to our relations in Minorca. She no doubt hoped they would give her refuge, her and little Edi. But the dear relations were not interested, presumably they thought they had already done their bit for Christian charity with me. They were nevertheless so kind as to let Marga know that I could be contacted at the address of my parents-in-law, 16 Calle Embajadores, Madrid, and my sister sent me a message hoping I would help her. But how was I supposed to help her, I was in a bad way myself, I was behind bars. When her letter reached Madrid, I had already been arrested. My mother-in-law read it out to me in Segovia, in the women's prison, in visiting time. Fernando was also behind bars. And his mother was looking after our boy. Julián was not even two yet. One year and eleven months.

I was twenty-one years and ten months, when our transport arrived at the camp, on 6th October 1942, nine months after Rudi Friemel, of whose existence I had no idea at the time. How should I have known him? Vienna isn't a village, I'm thirteen years younger than he is, and until then I had not been much interested in politics. I did, however, have a well-developed sense of justice, even as a child, and more than once drove my mother to despair because of it. But I never joined a party. My father was Jewish, and because there were not supposed to be marriages between members of different confessional groups, my mother, who came from a Baptist family in Dresden, adopted the Jewish faith. I was only three when they separated and conducted a bitter struggle for custody of me. My stepfather, whom I liked very much, was a well-known defence lawyer. He died early, and that was the end of affluence at home. My mother was still able to pay for grammar school up to fourth year, then I had to leave. Right after that my grandmother was knocked down by a car, and I went to Dresden for three months to look after her. Apart from one uncle who was an in-law, all my mother's brothers and sisters were dyed-in-the-wool Nazis, two of them since the early 1920s. But that didn't stop them liking me. The neighbours were still friendly to me as well; first of all, they had known me since I was a baby, second, they regarded me as a foreigner, for whom what happened in Germany was of no significance, third, the district where my grandmother lived had been a Communist stronghold and was still fairly resistant to the Nazis.

After my return my mother fixed me up as a clerical apprentice in the Goldscheider ceramics factory. There I learned such useful things as fetching the mid-morning snacks for the other employees, making tea or coffee, dusting the typewriters and office furniture and stacking old files in the cellar. Is that all, I thought, and broke off the training without further ado. Now my mother wanted to put me in a private commercial school. The plan was postponed for a year because I had to take care of my grandmother in Dresden again. I finally started the school in autumn 1937, but the pleasure only lasted one semester. On the evening of 11th March 1938 I had arranged to meet a friend in Café Börse. The wireless was on somewhere in the background, we didn't pay any attention to it until the programme was interrupted just before eight. 'I declare before the world.' It was Schuschnigg's farewell speech. Yield to force, on no account shed German blood, German word of honour, dearest wish, and God save Austria. We left the café in a complete daze. The Ringstrasse was already closed off with rolls of barbed wire. Still that same night I accompanied my mother to Café Herrenhof, down to the dance cellar, where my mother wanted to warn her Jewish friends. Firemen were just tearing down the banners of the Fatherland Front, calling for a yes to Austria. At the corner of Schottengasse a dark-haired man came towards us, he was wearing glasses and had a somewhat large nose, and another man, a Nazi with a swastika armband, pounced on him, you Yid pig, I'm going to get you, and hit him in the face, so that his glasses flew off in a wide arc. The dark-haired man grabbed the thug by his tie, clouted him twice and said quite calmly: I'm not a Yid, nor even a Yid pig, but for the blow you wanted to give a Jew, you've now got two in return. Then he bent down for his glasses, put them on and walked away.

The next morning I went to school. Several fellow-students had already arrived at the entrance in Rauhensteingasse, which was cordoned off by Nazi brownshirts. It was said, the commercial school was being blockaded because the owners, the Allina brothers, were Jews. We stood around for one and a half hours not knowing what to do, then we set off home. There was a sign in the window display of Lehmann's cake shop on the Graben: 'No Jews or dogs allowed', and further on I already saw Jews kneeling in the road, with laughing and howling passers-by forcing them to rub away the Austro-Fascist cross with toothbrushes. Later that same day the doorbell rang, and outside stood yet another man with a swastika armband and demanded to see the Yid pig Kurt Rosenfeld, that is, my stepfather, at which my mother with a harsh laugh said: Then you'd better get down to the Central Cemetery, Gate Four, he's been there since 1931.

On the top floor there was a carpet mender by the name of Tesar. Just a couple of weeks before, he had announced to the grocer opposite that with three party membership books – those of the Social Democrats, the Christian-Socials and the illegal Nazi Party – he was prepared for all eventualities; now he was busy relieving the Wassermann family on the first floor of jewellery, silver and wall clock. We were lucky, because a brother of my mother, who had participated in the invasion as a soldier, took up quarters with us four days later and that made quite an impression in the house. Uncle Alfred was shocked by the outrages, which outdid in their brutality everything that he had seen in Germany. Nothing will happen to you, he said to my mother, but Dagmar has a Jewish father. For the time being I would be safer away from home, in the old Reich, under the protection of the family.

When he left Vienna again on his motorbike I went with him in the sidecar, disguised in an army coat and cap. For two years I worked in a clothing factory in Dresden without the least problem, then I was drafted to work in the Zeiss-Ikon plant, in a separate Jewish section, had to wear the Jews' star and move into a segregated Jewish apartment. A Gestapo officer, who was constantly harassing me, warned me to refrain from any contact with Jewish or Aryan men. But my undoing proved to be the woman with whom I was lodged, whose daughter worked in the same place as I did. Under interrogation by the secret police she let slip that I had talked to my mother from a public telephone – which as a half-Jew I was strictly forbidden to do. In August 1942 I too was summoned to the Gestapo. The officers assured my uncle, who had accompanied me in his army uniform, that I would only be held for a week. The cell in the Gestapo prison filled up, there was no more talk of release. One night at the end of September I was called to sign my preventive detention order. I found myself in the prison at Alexanderplatz, in Berlin, then in Ravensbrück. A big Jewish transport left the camp three days later.

It was a normal passenger train, the doors were locked and SS men installed themselves at either end of the carriage. We travelled across flat countryside, it seemed sombre and naked to me, at a station where water was taken on, Polish voices could be heard between the crunching of the sentries' boots, and suddenly the word was mentioned, the key word. I only realised its significance after our arrival, when early in the morning, between four and five, we were chased into a barbed-wire square by a dog team.

We had to line up in ranks, SS men in front of us, among them one who was a good six foot six inches, and behind them barracks and sheds, and between and in front of the barracks figures were scurrying around, shadowy, with shaven heads, a men's camp, I thought, they've brought us to a men's camp, and gradually it grew light, gradually I grew weak, stick it out, in a moment they'll dismiss us, and then a hill emerged in the pale greyness, almost as tall as one of these huts, and the hill was made of brushwood, strange, all these branches, and the grey grew brighter, I saw, something was moving in the brushwood, there's something stirring, I whisper, and the lips of the girl beside me are trembling, silently, and then I see the brushwood, the branches, the mountain of corpses, scrawny, bony corpses, stacked up, no, thrown on top of each other, but now they were all dead, nothing has moved.

Go on, go on, get moving! shouted the SS men, as our transport reached the railway station of the place, sixteen months after Rudi's arrival. It was pitch dark, it was night, there was a black-out in force. They drove us to the camp at a trot, where, outside the wall, we were locked into the reception building, which at that time was still under construction. Only at daybreak were we marched through the gate. Into a block, then showering, hair cropping, registration. Grabbing clothes, slipping into wooden clogs. The transformation from enemy of the people into a number. But it would be wrong to assume that we immediately grasped the full extent of the horror. Yet we were not unaware. We knew in outline what things were like in the concentration camps. I had known it since 1933, when I had read in Austrian newspapers that there people are tormented to death or killed, but that officially the word is: shot while attempting to escape. (But I didn't know the SS men's favourite game, throwing caps – the victims were shot when they were ordered to retrieve them.) I also knew that prisoners who attempted to escape were hung. (But letting them starve to death in the standing cell, the shots in the back of the head at the Black Wall, the Boger Swing during interrogation, that I didn't know.) I also think that I heard during the transport about the extermination of the Jews. A fellow-prisoner had claimed that Thomas Mann had spoken on American wireless broadcasts about it. But perhaps my memory is deceiving me, that's why I distrust it: It mixes what one has experienced and what one has heard, does not stick to any sequence, doesn't obey the calendar, but the seasons. Hence in my memory I have retained the day, which always comes to mind when I think of Rudi Friemel, as a typical All Saints' Day: cold and grey, with bare branches, occasional snowflakes. At any rate at the beginning my horror remained within bounds. Only with time did I discover where I actually was.

We spent the first few days in the quarantine block. A couple of political prisoners used every excuse to make contact with us. It was from them I heard for the first time that there were gas chambers. I had reckoned with blows, kicks, also with the gallows. But not with that. And the second shock came with the certainty: The SS gives prisoners injections to kill them. Phenol injections. However: Auschwitz is not just Auschwitz. In the official camp terminology the Stammlager − main camp − in which I, and before me Rudi Friemel, found myself, was a Grade 1 camp. So unlike Birkenau it was not a mass extermination camp. As a so-called Aryan one could, with a bit of luck and skill, survive Auschwitz 1. Apart from that we were privileged; as Reich Germans we were at the top of the Nazis' hierarchy, higher even than the Czechs and the west Europeans, French and Belgians, who in turn had better chances of survival than Yugoslavs and Poles, to say nothing of Russians. We were allowed to receive letters and even packages. We understood what the SS men were shouting. It was to our advantage if the sound of our voices reminded them of their childhood. Also important was the solidarity of the political prisoners. When I got there representatives of many nations already belonged to the resistance movement, the Combat Group Auschwitz, as we called it, not only Poles and Austrians. It met in Block 4, in a partitioned space under the cellar stairs, in which buckets, brushes and cloth rags were kept. The mere fact that one of the politicals approached someone, and told him how he had to behave, could save a life. I came to Auschwitz as a law student. While I was still in the quarantine block a graphic artist from Vienna impressed upon me not to give my profession as student to the committee which assigned us to work details but to say painter and decorator. But I had never held a paintbrush in my hand in my life. So what, he said, you'll soon learn, and if you don't no one will notice. As a result I was assigned to a good work detail; I didn't have to work outside, got around a lot, was soon able to get hold of razor blades or reels of thread, which could be swapped for socks or cubes of margarine, and was regarded by the SS as a skilled worker, whose life was more valuable than most others.

Rudi Friemel didn't even need to lie. As a car mechanic he was sitting pretty. Perhaps he worked in the SS Motor Transport Pool from the start. His work party was outside the actual camp, behind the Block Leader room. It was a long wooden barrack hut with a corrugated iron roof in a fenced-in area, in which maintenance work was carried out on trucks, cars and motorcycles. In autumn '44 there were even wrecked tanks of the SS Hitlerjugend Division, which were to be made operational again. The transport pool was a top work party. Friemel sat at the steering wheel himself, he started and ran in the vehicles. It is quite possible that the work party commander was also a car mechanic. Then they would have been colleagues, the SS man would soon have recognised that Friemel was very well qualified. He would have respected him, especially as Friemel was confident, not arrogant, but not humble either. I remember that once an SS sergeant from the electricians' work detail, who had a motor boat on the Sola, came to him: Look, my boat's not moving. Take a look at it. You know something about engines. And the two of them went out and down to the river, and Rudi stripped down the engine and put it together again, and then he started it and the two of them gave a shout of delight that you could hear from a long way off. I also remember that he slipped me women's underwear and bread when I was ordered to Birkenau, to paint numbers on huts and slogans like: 'A louse means your death' or 'There is only one road to freedom. The milestones are: Hard work, patriotism, cleanliness, obedience...' Rudi wasn't like some of the other camp VIPs, who hoarded their treasures, and you were sorry if you ever asked them for a favour. He was well-known, liked, a figure: That's someone who can help you. Once, on a Sunday afternoon, he gave me a handful of drugs, for sick Austrians who had arrived on a transport. Drugs! In the camp someone who had an aspirin was regarded as wealthy.

In the transport pool the rations were better, probably they were able to get something from the SS kitchen, and Friemel looked well-fed, as did Vesely, a cheerful youngster, who did clerical work there, a kind of adjutant to Friemel, the two were said to be insep- arable, and it seems to me that Friemel felt somehow responsible for the young fellow, who perhaps reminded him of his own youth. Anyway, Friemel was in good spirits, he was optimistic, he was a physically powerful man with a firm belief that there is a prospect of surviving this hellish camp. A committed Marxist, his morale absolutely firm, he didn't join the Party out of expedi- ency, but broke with the politics of the Socialists and declared for the CP out of profound conviction. When, I don't know. Proba- bly in 1941, after the German attack on the Soviet Union. So not because he expected something in return. In any case: Friemel was a Communist. Ernst Burger, whom I liked very much, because he was a bright working-class lad, told me about Friemel and his work, that Friemel was performing an important task, providing the others with information, because he had the opportunity to hear the wireless.

Later Friemel described the mood in the transport pool to me. They had a relatively good relationship with the SS men, that arose with time, and there was a terrible tendency to heavy drinking. Once they had nothing to drink, I remember it as if he had only told me yesterday, so the criminal prisoners drank methyl alcohol, which they made from petrol or petroleum, some kind of mixture. Two went blind as a result, and a couple of others ended up in the hospital and died. That was a consequence of the demoralisation, of the hopelessness that spread among the Germans after the defeat of Stalingrad.

When I was transferred to Auschwitz in August 1942, he was already there. In Dachau a fellow-countryman had told me, listen, in Auschwitz there's someone who can help you get your bearings, that's Ernst Burger. I became clerk in the hospital, where they had a huge card index, I found Burger in it. After a couple of days I went to look for him. He had fallen ill with abdominal typhus at the time, but was discharged by the Polish nurses, because they suspected that a selection was coming, and so he was in his block. I visited him there, in Block 4, at first he wasn't able to talk, but then he told me, there are two Austrians, Ludwig Vesely and Rudi Friemel, they can be relied on. From time to time we were able to have a short conversation. Friemel slept in a block where there were lots of Frenchmen. They liked him a lot. Incidentally, he was also much liked by the Poles.

Friemel once gave me new courage at a time when I was in complete despair and close to going to the wire, because I couldn't see any other way out. Don't do it, he said, hold out. Don't leave us alone. It is to this plea – and my wish not to refuse it – that I owe my life.

I didn't know this Friemel man, and I wouldn't have wanted to get to know him. To go by everything that I did know about him, he was imperturbable, calm, strong, pumped full of comradeship. Says: Consolation and resistance, and really thinks both are possible in this place, which I've never been able to rid myself of. So that you understand what I mean, I'll take you with me to the ramp. That's a privilege, don't forget it, you owe it to the fact that I've taken a fancy to you. I've spoken to the kapo, he's put you on the list. So unlike me your deployment doesn't need to cost you too much, such as promises of favours or barters in return, which are beneath your dignity. I'll show you everything you need to know. The glittering heat and the hellish thirst. The brisk march past the huts, at the double on the country road, the order: At ease!, the wait in the narrow shadow of the embankment. The tight cordon, the railway track above us, the tall chestnuts all around. The motorbikes on which the NCOs came roaring up, the canteen where they while away the time, with Apollinaris mineral water and family photos that pass from hand to hand. The growing tension, as we catch sight of our prey: the first goods waggons appearing round the bend, the engine right at the back, the long drawn-out penetrating whistle, the thick cloud of steam. The pale faces with wide-open eyes behind the small barred windows. The hammering of fists, from inside against the planks, and the cries, for water and air. The brief burst from the sub-machine gun, over the top of the trucks, which makes them fall silent. The rattle of the sliding doors, the pushing and shoving of those cooped up inside. The order, they should take their baggage with them and put it down in front of the trucks. The fearful questions of the new arrivals, even as they're still gasping for air, to which we don't respond or answer with another question: Where have you come from? The rapidly growing piles of suitcases, bags, rucksacks, satchels, coats and jackets. The whistle of the SS men's riding crops, their briefcases which receive gold and jewellery. The towers of bread, hams, sausage, the jars of jam and pickled vegetables gleaming in the sun. The uproar. The weak, who stumble and are trampled on. The handbags, banknotes, watches. The shrieks of the women, the crying of the children. The embarrassed silence of the men. The Red Cross van which races past with its cargo of poison gas. Our hardest work, clearing the trucks of the children, who have suffocated and been trampled to death, the cripples and the old. The equanimity with which we grab the little corpses by the neck, arm or leg and toss them out onto the ramp. The satisfaction that everything is going so smoothly. The fury that rises in us, as we observe a young woman out of the corners of our eyes. The woman, who suspects what is in store for mothers and children, and so hurries forward, anywhere away from the revving lorries, away from her little chubby-cheeked daughter, who toddles behind her sobbing. Mama, mama. You or me, who shouts at the woman. Will you pick up that child! The woman, who is healthy and beautiful. It's not my child! You or me, who pushes her to the ground, but even as she's falling pulls her up by the hair. Bitch. Running away from your own child. You or me, who with unexpected strength hurls her onto the lorry, and the child after her. Our fury next, at a girl who jumps from the third waggon and looks round inquiringly, then tosses her heavy dark hair out of her face and asks you or me: Look, where are we being taken? Her batiste blouse, her skirt, which she smooths straight, the thin golden watch on her wrist.

Her intelligent brown eyes. Why don't you say something. Your and my furious silence. Her proud sentence: I know, and her elastic steps, as she goes towards the lorry, pushes away the hand that tries to hold her back, and jumps up the steps. You or me, who follows her with his eyes. The red-painted fingernails on her hair flying in the headwind. Then back to the bending down and pulling, corpses, corpses, pieces of luggage, children, running about the ramp like stray dogs. An old man in tails, with an armband, who wants to speak to the Herr Kommandant. His head, which hits the ground. A girl with only one leg, who is carried over. You and me, who hold her by the hands and leg. Oh, that hurts, gentlemen. You and me, who throw her over to the corpses, to the old man in tails. Another girl, two or three years old, who leans right out after the opening of the seventh waggon door, loses her balance and falls head first onto the ballast, lies there stunned for a while, then gets up and spins round in a circle, ever faster. Her arms, which beat like wings, her mouth, which gasps for air, her monotonous whimpering. An SS man, who gives her a kick. The way the little girl falls, the way he presses her to the ground with his boot, draws his pistol, fires twice. The flailing of the thin legs, the way they're dragged over the ballast. The next waggon, the waiting, the next transport. The sunset, the twilight, the sparkling of the stars, the waning of the stars. The fading of the rage, the anticipation of what's left over for us. The order, march back to camp. Our kapo, who stuffs silk, gold and coffee into a big kettle, for the guards at the gate, so that they let us pass without inspection. Me, who slips into a pair of leather shoes, you, who have got hold of a silk shirt. Me, who slips a salami up his left sleeve. You, who secretly keeps hold of the pills, which you will exchange for two lemons and a used toothbrush, and at some point they'll end up with Friemel, who will pass them on as a present, before he services the lorries, which are needed for the next transport. Here there are no heroes, that's all I wanted to show you. And to make clear to myself, why I hate him so much, him and his wife and their wedding here, here in our Auschwitz home.

First we moved to Rotterdam. Then to Amsterdam. Then the Germans invaded. Then we set out one night to cross over secretly to England, but the freighter was hopelessly overcrowded, and we were afraid. When we returned, I put my little son to bed. The next morning he was quite happy and immediately started talking about our excursion to the coast and about the other people who wanted to flee, and about the boat which, in the end, we hadn't boarded. Then my husband said, you only dreamed it all, and my son contradicted him, and I too said, it was a dream, and then he looked at me, and I held his gaze, a dream that you cannot tell anyone, and he smiled and said, you're right, it was only a dream. Many officers came to our furrier's, they didn't care in the least that we were Jews, all that mattered was that they got what they were looking for, mink, Persian lamb, silver fox, for their wives and girlfriends at home, but when the campaign against Russia began, my husband was supposed to supply fur waistcoats to the German army on a large scale, and that was the moment we said to ourselves, now or never. The idea was for us to make our way to Spain, and from there take a ship overseas, because my brother-in-law had meanwhile obtained Cuban visas. He also found a German who regularly drove to France on Wehrmacht business and who declared himself prepared to smuggle us as far as Paris. That couldn't be done all at once. The men went first, with my son, the women the next day with the other children.

My son cried, as I pulled him from his bed at six in the morning. It was pouring with rain outside, time was short, so I put our big black umbrella in his hands, and at last he stopped crying. We crossed the Belgian border in the boot of a car. In Brussels we switched to a lorry. The driver hid us in the space behind the load, which consisted of a thousand cartons of cigarettes. The journey passed without incident. In Paris a young man was waiting for us. All of us together then travelled by train to a village a few miles from the demarcation line (between German-occupied France and Vichy-controlled territory). Immediately after our arrival our escort went to look for the driver of the postbus which travelled between the two parts of the country, we were to wait for him at an inn. A woman there looked us over and then got up and left, and I feared the worst, but I didn't say anything, so as not to disquiet the others, and what could we have done anyway. Then when our guide came back with the driver, we drove off right away, but didn't get far, because there was a German soldier standing in the middle of the road, who stopped the vehicle and ordered us to get out.

We were in Angoulême police prison for a couple of days, my husband and my brother-in-law in the men's wing, we women with my son in a cell with twenty others caught trying to cross the border illegally, then we were sentenced to ten weeks in prison and after serving our time were transferred to a camp. The sister of our escape helper had already taken my son before that, we learned she had placed him with a couple in Marseilles and that he was doing well there, that was a weight off my chest. Then all able-bodied men were deported, and a little later the women, the older men and the children were also transported. The waggon was so crowded that we couldn't turn. At every stop we begged for water. On the evening of the fifth day we reached the place.

The train continued a little way beyond the station, then we were driven out into the bright light with sticks. All women with children were taken away somewhere on lorries and I was over-joyed that I didn't have my son with me. On the fourth day on an outside work party, I wished I were dead, but on the evening of the tenth day I was still alive and was able to convince the block elder and then an SS major that I was a good clerk. So I found myself in the orderly room. Later I was transferred to the Political Section, to Registry Office II. Registry Office I was in the town and recorded births and marriages. Our section recorded only deaths. My job was to copy the death certificates with the fake causes of death into a big book. Until 1943 Jews too were registered individually, aside from those murdered in the gas chambers. With every transport from France I was choked with fear, I was tormented by the thought of finding the family from Marseilles who had taken in my son on the list of names, but finally one day I was holding his first letter in my hands, my brother had succeeded in getting him to Switzerland.

The interrogations also took place in our hut. I heard the pris-oners screaming, afterwards I saw them lying on the floor. The head of the Political Section was Maximilian Grabner from Lower Austria. Walter Quackernack from Bielefeld was in charge of the Registry Office, his deputy was called Bernhard Kristan and was from Königsberg.

Quackernack always acted very refined; when a court-martial was held he wore white gloves with his elegant uniform. Once I observed from my office window, as he took a children's transport to the gas chamber. When the children were herded from the lorries, a blonde little girl went towards Quackernack. I saw her raise her face towards him and ask something with a smile. I also saw how he kicked the girl with all his strength. She first of all lay there dazed for a moment, then she scrambled to her feet crying. I was crying too, I hadn't cried for a long time. Kristan loved killing. He was always in a good mood when he came back from executions. He also loved the pot plants in his office. Once he was gentle with a little cat. There's nothing better I can say about him. The two of them, Quackernack and Kristan, got very worked up, when two inquiries in quick succession came in. A registry office in Oldenburg was suspicious of the figures, they were reporting: 'It seems impossible that a small local authority like Auschwitz should be showing such a large number of deaths.' An office somewhere in Thuringia also suspected erroneous figures. The official there wondered whether the Auschwitz registry office was cumulatively including all the deceased since the introduction of civil registers in 1870. Quackernack avoided further objections, in that from then on he divided the number of dead in his reports by 180.

I was the last in this transport of 521 girls to be tattooed and got the number 21946. It's probably thanks to my big mouth that I didn't disappear up the chimney right away. When the transport list was read out, it turned out that my name was missing, and so I said to the SS man, well, if that's the case, then send me back home again. That didn't happen, but my cheek had evidently impressed him, because on his orders, after one day in the tree nursery outside detail I was transferred from Birkenau to Auschwitz, to the registry office. It was accommodated in a wooden hut next to the crematorium, and my task day after day was to draw lines on the death certificates with ink and a ruler.

My immediate superior was SS Sergeant Kristan, who looked as if he had walked out of an ancient Germanic saga. He could work himself into a rage about blond and blue-eyed Jews, and what he found especially detestable were half-Jews like me, who muddled up his concept of race. Kristan was the first one who wanted to hit me, that was with a folder. He had already raised his arm, but I looked him very steadily in the eye, and his eyes too became fixed, for seconds we stared at each other, then he lowered his arm. Much later, when the Spanish woman was brought into our office before the marriage ceremony, he was courtesy itself.

We had to marry because of the child, and it had to be in church, because Franco had prescribed a Catholic wedding as compulsory. But I wasn't baptised, and in order to save myself this piece of nonsense, I claimed I had been baptised in the Church of the Virgen de la Paloma, which had burnt out during the war. What a happy act of providence, exclaimed the priest of San Cayetano, to whom we gave notice of the intended marriage, the church is no longer standing, but thanks to the intercession of our Holy Virgin the parish register has survived unscathed! So that was that as far as my plan was concerned, so I had no choice except go through with the whole farce, baptism, wedding and baptism again, because Julián couldn't remain a heathen child. At first we lived with my parents-in-law, then we came into an inheritance and were able to afford an apartment in the Colonia Moscardó, on the other side of the Manzanares. That same month, July '43, Fernando managed to get a job in a bank. At this point I was already taking care of communication between the Party in Madrid and headquarters in France. It wasn't that I was desperate to do it. Other people had more sense than I did. But given the situation in those days, it wasn't just a matter of sense. Someone had to do it. And that was me. And at the end of July my brother sent this lad to us, Juan Ros, whom I knew from France. On 3rd August he was supposed to meet a contact in the Retiro Park. I couldn't stay at home that day, I had to take an urgent piece of information to a comrade in prison, encoded of course, Fernando had already gone to work, and so I said to Juan, I'll leave the boy here, when you go out, you take him to Fernando's cousin. And that's what he wanted to do, but the cousin wasn't at home, and he had to be in the Retiro at ten on the dot, so he simply took Julián with him. And in the park the police were waiting for him. If the boy hadn't been with him, Juan would no doubt have opened fire. They would have killed him, but one or more of them would have been dead first. He tried to play for time. Three times he sent them to a wrong address, but at the fourth they grabbed Julián by a leg and made as if to smash his head against the wall. Then he told them what they wanted to know. To me he had said, if I'm not back by four, you know what to do. He had brought a lot of leaflets with him. At ten to four they stormed the apartment. They didn't bother to ring first. When they opened the cupboard, the pile was already falling towards them.

Well, Marina, what's this then.

No idea, it belongs to our guest, I don't go snooping around in things that don't belong to me.

They didn't get any more out of me. I don't know anything, again and again. Come on, are you really so stupid. Yes, I'm stupid. And I stuck to that. Because it was clear to me, as soon as I start to talk, I'm lost. Say nothing and act dumb. They didn't know anything about me. I was married to the guy beside me, and his parents, decent people, were ordinary workers, on whom there was nothing. Fernando wasn't incriminated either. Even though they had a photo of him, with a moustache, taken in the street from the side, it looked as if one hand was missing. They asked me, who's the cripple, I've never seen him before, I replied, perhaps a friend of my husband. Then we had the good luck that the warder down in the cellar of the security police building was a secret Communist. He came into Fernando's cell, take this, brother, it'll do you good, and when Fernando opens the sandwich, he finds a scrap of paper and a pencil stub inside. Thanks to this comrade we were able to make our statements match. I wrote to Fernando that I had not admitted anything, and because he knew that, he didn't walk into any trap set by these idiots, who thought they were so smart, and their smartness was always making them trip over themselves. Today I can laugh about it. But then I was shaking with fear. Anyone who says they weren't afraid during the interrogations is lying. Even Fernando, who never admits to anything, says he was sweating blood, and not just a little. It was pure horror. Worse than fear.

They executed the lad, Juan Ros. On a Good Friday, as good Catholics. He was only twenty. I saw him just once more, in the courtroom. His face was disfigured by the tortures, I would hardly have recognised him again. He asked me to forgive him. There's nothing to forgive, my son. You did nothing wrong. You couldn't magic Julián away.

The public prosecutor also demanded the maximum sentence for me, paragraph 38 or 238. Firing squad, in other words. Fernando's mother, who until that day had always avoided priests, immediately ran off to the church and started praying non-stop. In the end Fernando and I got six years. Six years and one day, to be exact. Jesus Christ in person had already assured his mother beforehand that they wouldn't execute us. Once, when she visited me in hospital, she said: Set your mind at rest, nothing will happen to the two of you, I asked the Saviour of Medinaceli, and he shook his head. The poor woman believed that in all seriousness. That shows you what imagination can do to a person.

In prison I didn't give in either. Whether it was in Ventas, in Segovia or in Soria — there was always an opportunity to make life hell for the women warders. We were a good gang, Julia, Nieves, Lolita, La Peque, who got away in Segovia. The rope with which she climbed over the wall we twisted together from bits of string we wheedled from our relatives, for skipping, we told them. La Peque escaped one evening at nine, while the prison governess was maltreating the piano and the staff was reverently dozing. Then when we were counted, before lights-out, she was already miles away. The warders behaved like furies. One of the Reds has gone! Kill her, if you find her! Some time later she was picked up again and shot. That was 1945. Her real name was Asunción Cano.

Fernando was released in March '47. They kept me in a year longer for bad behaviour. No wonder, they put me in the punishment cell nine times. I was the first to throw a plate at their feet. The muck they gave us was full of worms. Hunger strike, then once again, because they were beating prisoners. At the beginning the warders still forced us to give the Fascist salute at roll call. And they got into a rage if they smelled the anisette, which we put into the clay jugs, just a couple of drops, so that the water didn't taste so much of the clay.

I replied to Marga's first letter, in which she poured out her heart to me, in four lines. Julián is healthy and cheerful, so far things are all right, Fernando's parents are well. How are you, what is Edi up to. Your sister Marina embraces you. I wasn't allowed to write more, the warders would have torn up the card and stopped me having visits, and I didn't want to involve my parents-in-law in the business, they were already saddled with enough. Marga couldn't write what she wanted either. Sometimes letters arrived, in which the censors had deleted whole paragraphs. Blacked out, one could only guess what was actually written there. She was desperately unhappy. Of course, she was having a hard time, but wasn't everyone having a hard time then? At least she was allowed to have her boy with her. I couldn't. A mother without her child, there's nothing worse than that. It's an unbearable pain. Be quiet, Fernando, it's not something a man understands. I had to live with it, I didn't have any choice. Julián, who said Mama to his grandmother, and when I was finally released, he was almost seven and didn't recognise me any more.

At some point she sent the wedding photograph. It's a good likeness, of both of them. A couple more good-looking than a pair of film stars. Margarita's face is sad, full of sorrow, but he's smiling. With the photo came the book, a novel by Pereda, *Penas arriba*. That was Rudi's present for me, he wrote a dedication: 'For my little sister-in-law Marina'. I've no idea how Marga managed to smuggle the book out of Auschwitz. She was very slim in those days, perhaps she hid it on her body, under her blouse. I read it probably a dozen times in Segovia, not because of the story, there's too much incense and nature in it for me, but because of him. Because of you, Rudi. I swear to you, I was never in love, but I never forgot you either. Fernando... he wasn't up to much, to look at, I mean. But when I realised what a good-hearted man he is, the way he looked didn't bother me any more.

Your book. Years later Julián brought a friend home, he pounced on it, I always wanted to read that, will you lend it to me. Of course, he never gave it back.

Margarita Ferrer has left few traces in Kirchheim unter Teck, that industrious little Swabian town. I was there, I looked around, and in the town hall was given a map and an information leaflet, which invites the reader to take a walk into the past, from St Martin's Church and back to the church square by way of twenty-three stations. The Wächter Home is not on the recommended route. It's on Schlierbacher Strasse, which leads to Wangerhalde and then continues in the direction of Göppingen. In 1961 the two-storey building, which had been used since 1894 as a care home for single girls pregnant for the first time, was completely renovated and several extensions were added. From the early thirties the home was also a maternity hospital for women from the town and the surrounding area; today the main focus is care of the elderly and youth welfare services. I imagine I recognise Margarita in a photograph printed in the brochure '100 Years Wächter Home Foundation', in the section about the years between 1933 and 1945. The picture caption refers to a mothers' day, there's a crowd of children, the girls with flowers in their hair, two nursing sisters from the deaconesses in Schwäbisch-Hall in cap and apron, and six mothers or helpers. The one in the middle, short hair, checked blouse, and smiling, that must be her. And the child in her arms seems to be smiling too. He has a prominent chin. Edi, I think.

Matron – that is, in charge of the Wächter Home – at that time was Sister Berta Wurst, a tenacious, determined woman evidently, who conducted a running battle with the National Socialist authorities over the ban on baptisms in the home. She was no support to Margarita. On the neighbouring Ziegelwasen there is the butcher Feinkost Kübler. Did the shop already exist then, and if so, did Margarita help out there from seven in the morning until eleven at night? I assume the wages to which she was entitled were kept back by the Wächter Home, offset against the costs of her accommodation and Edi's board, and she was always in the red.

The municipal archive is housed on the Freihof site, as it's called. Margarita's residence registration form and her residence certificate are preserved here. Surname Friemel, status married, nationality Spain. But the resident's registration card refers to a communication from the Stuttgart Municipal Welfare Office, according to which she is a German citizen. The Welfare Office in turn backs up its information by noting that on 26/8/1941 Frau Margarete Friemel received a green returnees' ID, which was only given to Germans.

So Margarita and Edi had first arrrived in Stuttgart. According to the residence registration form they were accommodated in the returnees' hostel there, the Hotel Central, Schlossgasse 16, before they were lodged in the Wächter Home in Kirchheim on 6th October. On that day the local paper, the *Teckbote* reported the favourable progress of military operations: in southern Ukraine more than 12,000 prisoners were taken, Britain was again the poorer by 56,000 tons of shipping and 476 aircraft, the Führer gave a rousing speech and founded the Military Order of the German Cross, Party District Leader Gross spoke in Weilheim about the significance of present-day events, in Linsenhofen a worker drew a prize of 500 Reichsmark at Kirchner's bookmakers, and VFB Kirchheim won a narrow but deserved victory over the Nürtingen team. On Monday 3rd May 1943 the *Teckbote* was both more muted in tone and thinner. A miner as 'pioneer of labour', all Bolshevik attacks repulsed, oak leaves for a brave staff sergeant, earthquake in southwest Germany.

The night-time earthquake, which on the Schwäbische Alb

registered seven on the twelve-point Mercalli Scale, affected the whole of Württemberg and Baden. Clocks stopped, bedsteads and heavy wardrobes shifted, doors burst open, vases fell from tables, cattle bellowed in their stalls. Even if the epicentre had been right under the Wächter Home, Margarita would only have felt the occurrence as part of a larger catastrophe; her terror was of a different nature. On 3rd May 1943 she left the town with Edi; according to the resident's registration card her next stop was Vienna, 10th District, 10 Ernst Ludwig Gasse.

That is all that is known about her in Kirchheim unter Teck. Despair is not for the record.

I already knew Rudi before I saw him for the first time. There was a fat confidential file on him, from which it emerged that he had fought on the side of the revolutionaries in the war in Spain and had also married there. The marriage ceremony was not recognised by the authorities, and he did all he could to be allowed to marry his wife again. With this end in view he often had an appointment with the head of the Political Section, and then with Quackernack or Kristan as well. None of them could resist his winning character for long. He always had a friendly smile for us, and if there was no SS man in the room, he asked if there was anything we needed, stockings or shoe polish or a piece of soap.

A friend of mine worked in the censor's office, and sometimes had the opportunity to read his letters to the Spanish woman. She could recite whole paragraphs from them by heart. So we shared in his love and were soon likewise in love. Rudi was fighting for the trust of his wife, perhaps it was that that overwhelmed us, in the middle of the dying all around and the death lists, which were more than we could cope with, and the certainty that, we the death clerks, would not survive. That was clear to us, Kristan and the others didn't even need to drum it into us: At best you'll die of old age here. But if you ever do get out, no one will believe you.

From Rudi's letters it was evident that the Spanish woman was disheartened and had decided to go back to her own country. He was afraid that he would lose her and their son for ever, tried to make her change her mind and promised her 'the fulfilment of your summer night's dream in Sillingy'. What kind of dream could that have been, we asked ourselves, on a mild French night at the edge of a field, on a camp street, leaves rustling, crickets chirping, sweet scent of hay or burnt flesh. Down in the valley the lights of the village, of the arc lamps, are shining into the cellar of the administration building. Or a summer night in the room on the market place, quiet babble of voices from the window opposite, a peal of laughter sometimes, the curtain billowing out, the rustling of clothes hanging in the darkness and the dream of the hand at my throat, from which I wake with a start bathed in sweat, the moaning, the weeping on the plank beds around me and a profound feeling of security, that makes one believe wishes come true. We could not get enough of it. Not of the worries, not of the dreams, not of the words of endearment. My poor brave wife! My beloved Spanish woman! My dear, dear Marga! Sweet little love! Our life, and how beautiful it will be. Do not be downhearted, be patient, I'm proud of you and of Eduardito, who looks like me, but has your eyes, and they bear their sunny homeland in their gaze (a photo of the boy, which she sent him, which we didn't see). I know, he wrote, that you want to get out of your difficult situation, and it is with sadness, that I feel that you want to go far away from me with our little son – but I cannot do anything else except say to you: Stand firm, and fight with me for our future together. It's the hardest part of the path, but the last before our goal.

Stand firm, we wrote too in our thoughts, don't go back to Spain, I love you both terribly much, Marga, believe him, and when we meet again, there will be a party like never before; you just have to see it through, no matter how hard it is.

So many embraces, such great longing, such beautiful big dark eyes. A thousand kisses.

It's unclear to me, how Margarita Ferrer could have managed to come by the green returnee's card. Perhaps she was not as help-less as it seems. Or perhaps it was only due to a clerk's mistake and to the inattentiveness of her superior, who absent-mindedly signed the document. Margarita, after all, couldn't provide any-thing as proof. In his petition to Reich Security Head Office in Berlin, which he submitted on 29th April 1942, Rudi Friemel maintains that he married her in January 1939. That marriage, however, like many others, was declared invalid by the subsequent Spanish government. The only marriage document, an attestation issued by the local military authority, had gone missing in the course of subsequent events. He had not wanted to marry in France, but in his homeland, to which he had returned with wife and child at the first opportunity. As urgent reason for his request, Friemel gives Margarita's intention, should the present situation continue, of returning to Spain with their son, which would rob him of the possibility of having the child educated in his home-land and of legalising the family circumstances. 'Through attain-ment of Reich German citizenship through marriage my wife would be in a position to go to my parents in Vienna, in order to live there and take up employment, so that her livelihood and that of the child would be secure, until I myself am able to assume care of both.'

Even before that, Clemens Friemel had attempted to achieve official recognition of the marriage. He wrote to the Reichsstatthalter – Reich Governor – in Vienna. The latter considered it imperative, so as to clarify the facts of the case, to establish Margarita's nationality, and instructed the District Administrator of Nürtingen to order the above-mentioned to send the marriage certificate to Vienna at the earliest opportunity. The District Administrator forwarded the instruction to the mayor of Kirchheim unter Teck, who directed the Municipal Document Office accordingly, which in turn applied to the Municipal Welfare Office in Stuttgart, which sought advice from the Section for Germans from Abroad, which confirmed Margarita's assertion as fact: Frau Friemel had acquired German nationality through marriage in 1939 and had been given Returnee Card no. 14779 by the Stuttgart Office of the Foreign Organisation. The mayor of Kirchheim unter Teck thereupon wrote to the District Administrator in Nürtingen that Frau Friemel was unable to provide the marriage certificate, because her marriage had apparently not been recognised by the National Government in Spain, so he requested that the matter not be pursued any further. Kirchheim unter Teck, 24th August 1942.

The matter was indeed not pursued any further. Because on 16th December 1942 Rudi Friemel handed in a second petition in which he once again expressed his fear of losing wife and child. In a letter of the 10th of the same month, Margarita had asked him to consent to her going home. He had neither the right nor the possibility of refusing her. In this desperate situation he most urgently requested a positive consideration of his petition of 29th September, or at least a concrete response with respect to his plea.

He will attempt to persuade his wife to postpone her decision until then.

In the spring of 1943 a positive or at least encouraging response must have been received, since on 3rd March Friemel writes in a letter to his father, that the matter – 'as you can see from the enclosed lines to Marga' – has made considerable headway. These lines are not preserved; it can only be assumed that the headquarters office in Berlin approved Margarita's move to Vienna and has requested the submission of various personal documents in order to process the petition. Friemel tried hard to rebut all conceivable objections to the move on the part of his father and stepmother – Clemens Friemel had married again two years earlier; Marga would certainly not make any financial demands on the couple, since labour was in short supply. 'The main worry remains the child and accommodation. If M. is working in a factory, how would the child be looked after? If the little one is in a home, can she see him every day or even take him back to where she's living? With respect to an apartment: what concrete possibility is there?'

Evidently his father was very reserved about the business. In a biographical sketch, which she wrote down years later, Margarita mentions a letter in which Clemens Friemel advised her not to come to Vienna for lack of anywhere to stay. She tore up the letter, sent a telegram, in which she informed him of her time of arrival, and, with Edi, caught the next train. In Vienna she quickly found work in the armaments industry, but the accommodation problem remained unsolved, until finally Frau Vesely took pity on her. In a letter of 11th September 1943, Ludwig Vesely had asked his mother to take in Margarita and the child: He and Rudi were good friends: 'We work together, sleep next to one another, share everything, in short we are comrades, such as are only found at the front, or somewhere else where there is privation.'

The matter dragged on for another six months. Both in his letters to Marga as in his petitions to Reich Security Headquarters, Friemel kept his emotions under control. I have the impression that he weighed up every word very carefully before he put it down in writing. He didn't try to ingratiate himself, made no concessions to the practices of National Socialist correspondence. Only to his father did he now and then hint that he was at the end of his tether. In an undated letter, presumably of December 1943, Friemel wrote to Vienna, he would make another appointment to see the camp commandant; 'if nothing comes of that, then I'm finished with *everything*. I only feel sorry for M., who has suffered so much for nothing.' Five weeks later the longed-for approval arrived; Friemel's second petition, to be allowed to travel to Vienna for the marriage ceremony, was not, however, granted. On 6th March 1944 the registry office official wrote on behalf of Kristan to Clemens Friemel: 'According to a comunication from Auschwitz Concentration Camp, Reich Security Headquarters Berlin has granted permission for you and your son Klemens to attend the marriage ceremony as witnesses. So that you have time to make all the arrangements I have, in agreement with your son, postponed the ceremony to 18th March 1944 at 11 am. I would ask you to arrive punctually. Your son Klemens was notified by me, Frau Ferrer y Rey by Auschwitz Concentration Camp.'

She didn't tell me anything about it. But from conversations that my mother had with neighbours and acquaintances, I knew that he was imprisoned. In a camp, the name of the camp was never mentioned. It wasn't necessary – I knew which side we were on. I wasn't in the Hitler Youth, for example. My mother didn't allow it. A letter came once, in which I was threatened with reprisals, if I didn't report to them within a week. Hardly had I got there, than they formed a squad and beat me up on the spot. So I said to myself, you want to have me, no way!

My mother didn't sympathise with the Nazis at all, quite the contrary. She listened illegally to foreign broadcasts whenever she could and commented on the speeches of Party bosses with barbed remarks. My Uncle Klemens was the only member of the Friemel family with whom she was still occasionally in contact. He lived with a woman, Reli, who had a daughter by another man. As a child I often visited them, they lived in a side street off Erdberger Strasse, they had a crystal set, they were always very nice. Klemens was also able to distract my mother with jokes, whenever she was angry with my grandfather. Later on he became very ill. He had boxed when he was young and sustained a foot injury which took a long time to heal. Because he limped, he was not called up for the Wehrmacht. He worked for the post office. I really only remember him telling jokes and clowning around. I can't remember any political remarks. No doubt he was influenced by the home he grew up in, so a Social Democrat, but not as active as the other men in the family. Perhaps my mother found out about the wedding from him. She knew about it at any rate.

Rudi Friemel is going to marry.

I was speechless.

Yes, he's going to get married, to a Spanish woman, by whom he already has a child.

Getting married in a concentration camp. Where everyone just dies.

And in Block 24, no marriage by proxy, his wife is going to come here specially, and a proper registrar is going to marry them, and she will spend one day here in the camp, and so the child will also have a father.

A legitimate father, that was tremendously important in those days.

Then I also heard: We're going to make him a wedding present! A white shirt is being embroidered.

One day we were told: A Spanish woman, a civilian, is coming here now, she's marrying Rudi Friemel. Immediately after that she was led in by an SS man. She looked just as one imagines a typical Spaniard, narrow face, black hair, black eyes. She was wearing a dark suit, underneath it a white blouse. On her head she had a little white hat with little flowers. Someone offered her a chair, but she remained standing. She was embarrassed and agitated, and she didn't say a word. Probably it had been impressed on her not to talk to us. I assume she was brought to the typing room because there was not much to be seen here of what went on in the camp. Unlike the interrogation rooms.

Then Friemel came over from the men's camp. He was dressed for the occasion, in suit, shoes and tie from the SS clothes store. They didn't embrace. They were awkward, both of them, and didn't really know where to put themselves. Quackernack seemed self-conscious too; to cover up his uncertainty, he insisted that time was pressing. Come on, let's go.

This is the first time that I've heard that Friemel's brother and his father and also his child were present at the marriage ceremony. I didn't see them in our typing room at any rate. It's possible that they waited in the town, or outside in front of the barrack building. On the other hand I can't imagine them leaving a whole family standing there. Perhaps they waited outside the fence, beside the camp commandant's villa.

As clerk in the SS precinct I had a pass, which permitted me to enter the camp without a guard as escort. I always carried a briefcase, stuffed with papers, in order to make an impression in the event of checks. It was the same that day, a beautiful early spring day, which was as if made for the occasion. I knew, it's the wedding day, but hadn't given it another thought, and walked through the gate at some point, when exactly, I don't know, at any rate the camp was fairly empty, and there I see a woman walking with a child and I think, that must be them. I didn't say anything, they were accompanied by an SS man, after all. Perhaps I whispered something. *Felicidades*. And I patted the boy's head, I'm quite certain of that.

Instead of Quackernack, who had been transferred, Kristan deputised as registrar. He made sure that Friemel was able to appear in front of his family in time. We were as excited as if we were to be married ourselves and crowded round the windows when the couple walked to the exit, followed by the father and the brother of the bridegroom, with the child between them. Kristan and an SS man concluded the ceremony. The marriage was carried out once more in accordance with German law at the registry office of the town of Auschwitz. Shortly afterwards the wedding party returned to our section. While his father and brother said goodbye, Kristan sent our head clerk to the conductor of the prisoners' orchestra, which was to play for the newlyweds. Because the camp commandant had not been asked for permission beforehand, the concert did not take place.

Wrong three times over! First of all, it was a Spaniard who got married. He had defended Madrid, then he had escaped to France, there he had found himself a French woman and had a child by her. Then the Germans caught him and brought him here. When the child was a bit bigger and the Spaniard was still in the camp, the French woman started clamouring that she wanted to be married. So a petition was sent off to Herr Reichs-führer SS Himmler in person. Himmler was indignant: Is there no order in the new Europe? Marry them immediately! Second, they promptly shipped the French woman, together with the child, to the camp, where they hurriedly pulled the striped clothes from the Spaniard's back. They stuck him in an elegant suit pressed personally by the camp kapo in the laundry room, put a matching tie around his neck, and so the wedding could be enacted. Third, the orchestra certainly did play after the marriage ceremony, when the newlyweds were sent to have their wedding pictures taken by the records department: she with a bunch of hyacinths and the child in her arms, he with his chest swelling with pride. Behind them marched the orchestra, playing for all they were worth, unperturbed by the SS man in charge of the kitchen, who was scolding like a fishwife: Playing music during working hours instead of peeling potatoes! I'll pay you back for this! I've got the soup ready and there are no potatoes! You can all lick... His cronies tried to calm him down: It's orders from Berlin. We can have soup without potatoes for once. The pictures of the newly-weds had meanwhile been taken, and the couple were allowed to withdraw to the camp brothel which had been cleared for the one night. The next day the French woman was chased back to France, and the Spaniard was back on a work party wearing his threadbare jacket. But now everyone in the camp walks around proudly, head held high, as if they had swallowed a ramrod: Here in our Auschwitz home we even have weddings.

The camp brothel was accommodated in Block 24, on the first floor. It consisted of eighteen cells, in which twelve German and six Polish tarts performed their duty. Most of the women wore the black triangle, they had already worked as prostitutes before. But there were also some who had volunteered out of sheer desperation. The food was better, and at night the men brought little presents with them. There was the case of a seventeen-year-old girl, who begged the head of Birkenau women's camp, SS captain Hössler, to assign her to the brothel. She had not yet slept with a man but in order to save her life was now firmly determined to do so. Hössler was so moved by his own compassion that he had the girl transferred to a different work detail. In another case a Pole, as he was marching back from work one evening, saw his wife sitting in the brothel window. Until then he hadn't even known that she was in the camp.

Among the political prisoners it was considered dishonourable to go to the camp brothel. One needed a coupon, which had to be handed in at the door. The kapos only gave coupons to those who had organised something for them. In the reception room sat an SS man with the rank of medical orderly, who gave the customers an injection for syphilis. They had to be outside again in fifteen minutes. I knew what it was like there, because in autumn '43 our work detail had to paint the rooms. On the orders of the camp commandant a Jewish prisoner from Holland, a very talented artist, drew naked or half-naked women on the walls – whatever the Nazis imagined was erotic. I assume the SS thought it a great laugh, to put up the newlyweds in the brothel. It didn't bother us, on the contrary, the wedding was like immersing in a reality which we had long ago lost. We also chalked it up as a patriotic gain, as a kind of self-assertion, perhaps even as a belated correction of our defeats. We did not consider what a shattering effect it all must have had on our Polish comrades.

To both of you, Rudi!

Suddenly everything was quite different. We sat in the cellar of the clothes store, had covered the windows and locked the block door. There was something to eat. There was something to drink. I even lit myself a cigarette. His eyes shone. Ludwig was beaming too. How was it, Rudi, tell us at last, from the beginning and all in the order it happened.

Till death do you part.   ,

But that evening he was far away. I would never have thought of escaping. Anyone who escapes puts those left behind at risk. But late at night, as Ernst Burger and I walked down the camp street to our block, the decision was made. We would escape, because we knew now that we were alive. The wedding was the irrefutable proof of our existence.

3

THE SILENCE

She thinks about it sometimes, every day, at every minute, ever more rarely, even after forty years. Then something occurs to her again, but the closeness is gone, desire, being desired. Once she sits down, at night, her mind firmly made up. She listens hard, holding her breath. How happy she is at the silence. Nothing but the quiet, unthreatening glugging in the heating pipes. Her husband has already gone to bed. She would feel embarrassed, if he caught her writing. As if it were a betrayal of him, as if she should have a bad conscience, because of him and still because of her son, who grew up a long time ago. That's also why she finds it so difficult to find her way: because his shadow obscures Rudi's picture. And because the years since then have eaten away at the confidence, vitality, certainty that things will take the course, which she has longed for. She counts up: four complicated operations, high blood pressure, Edi's serious illness, which affected her very badly, the sudden death of her brother, the disappointing end of the great revolt, the lack of a genuine change in the country she comes from. And the worst thing of all, she writes, that one can suffer: the loss of trust in man's good nature, and the knowledge that ideals are no more than fantasies or rungs on a career ladder. With that – and with the fact that she's no longer twenty (twenty-nine when the war ended) – she excuses her muddled pathetic scribblings, which nevertheless tell of the great day, of the last night, of the absence. Nowhere, she writes, was I so unhappy.

Nowhere was I so unhappy as in this rough little town, with this grumbling, nagging butcher's wife, Frau something, to whom I was always only the dirty bitch, I've forgotten every German word, except those, and I wanted nothing more than to get away, somewhere, where I'm not a dirty bitch, but I couldn't, nobody wanted me and Edi, and in my exhaustion and isolation I agreed to go to Vienna. Rudi's father was against it, he wrote to me, his flat was far too small for all of us, but I set off nevertheless and in Vienna there was nothing to eat, in Vienna there was nothing to buy, in Vienna there was nothing to heat with, least of all for a foreigner with a child, and once I was shoved out of the tram, I was lucky there. The house was bombed, and Edi and I were the only ones who went on living in the ruin, but that was later, before that was the telegram. I didn't have anything to wear, and kind Frau Vesely, whom I'll never forget, took me to see her friend, the seamstress, who was so full of longing for her deported husband. It was in her tiny room that, for the first time in my life I saw a bed which, in a moment, with one flick of the wrist, is turned into a cupboard, and next to this bed-cupboard she sewed me the suit, and Frau Vesely gave me the nylon blouse as a present, which shimmered like raw silk, and for Edi the jumper and the trousers with straps, which he then wore. We had to spend the night before we left with my father-in-law, in order to be at the station in time, at dawn or after sunset, in the twilight at any rate, and, as once before, we had a compartment to ourselves. Edi slept on the bench next to me, he smiled in his sleep, and I was beginning to think we would never arrive.

There on the platform in the cold of the other town a soldier was waiting for us, whose duty it was to take us to the camp. We went on foot, no, we were taken there in a car, and at the edge of the road there were many women in thin smocks, digging ditches with pickaxe and spade, and I was ashamed to see their grey faces and red frozen hands. Then we got out and walked through the gate, I read the motto there and saw the wire and behind that the towers with the gun muzzles and in front the prisoners, looking at us, their suspicious eyes hurt me. After we had taken a couple of steps, the orchestra began to play, and the sound of the music drove me into the office, where officers in knee-boots were standing around. They said we should sit down on one of these office benches, in the first row, then we were called up by name, stepped forward and signed. Unexpectedly Rudi pulled two gold rings out of his pocket, one he put on my finger, the other I put on his. Now I flung my arms around him. Once Rudi's father and his brother had also signed the certificate, we were told the marriage ceremony had been performed.

When we left the office the orchestra played a march again, and it seemed to me that the eyes of the prisoners were already friendlier, as if the enemies of their enemies had won a victory. Then we went to the canteen, in which a table had been set only for us, and the prisoners who served the food whispered to me, how happy they were at this unique wedding. After the meal we looked over the rooms, which had been allocated to us for the night, one for my father-in-law and brother-in-law, the other for the three of us. As we went up the stairs, Rudi said, don't be cross because they've put us up here, because this is where the prostitutes are accommodated. In a long corridor on the first floor, with lots of doors going off it, there were several political prisoners waiting for us. They congratulated us, made jokes, and gave us drawings they had made just for this occasion. One of the prisoners was unusually big, well over six foot. He embraced us and pressed a bunch of flowers into my hand. It was the photographer, who then took the wedding pictures. Before he left, he gave me his parents' address. He asked me to visit them in Vienna, they should not worry about him, he was healthy and in good spirits. And I really did visit them, soon after our return, and told them everything, from then on they invited me and Edi to their home once a week, shared their meals with us and even gave me food packets.

After meeting his friends Rudi and I went for a long walk through the camp. On the way he told me what no one in Vienna knew, and whoever did know kept quiet: that here thousands upon thousands of Jews were being killed, in gas chambers, and when there was not enough gas, they were thrown into the fire. Rudi also confided to me that the secret resistance group was planning a break-out. He said, you have to understand that I'm joining them, even if I've married you, so that our child bears my name.

Chiquita, he said, in case something happens to me, in case we don't see each other again.

After supper we went up to our room. Rudi was mad about his boy, no wonder, Edi was a real rascal, bright, friendly and pretty as a picture with his curly hair. They played and romped around and tussled with one another, until finally Edi's eyes fell

shut. Rudi and I, we talked for hours after that. He was so different, and something was missing.

Next morning we had to get up early. The car that was to take
us to the station was already waiting. I had slept deeply, but Rudi
said he had lain awake all night. He was allowed to accompany us
to the gate, where he embraced his father, then his brother. Then
he kissed Edi, again and again. Finally he hugged me very tightly,
be strong, little woman, he whispered, turned abruptly away and
walked back into the camp. I watched him for a long time in the
hope that he would turn round once more.

I still had in my mind the picture of the twelve Poles who had
been hanged in July 1943. Their work party had been carrying
out survey work beyond the outer cordon, three men had used
this opportunity to escape. One evening the rest were dangling
from the crossbeam which had been screwed onto two solid
wooden posts in front of the kitchen barrack. On returning to
camp we had to pass them. They had yellow faces, unnaturally
stretched necks, threads of saliva were dribbling from their
mouths. So we knew, we weren't just risking our own lives. Nevertheless, the wedding had given us a lift, if the sanctions deterred
us, then we would never take any action. And it was high time,
the front was drawing ever closer, the Red Army could already
reach our area with their next offensive. Then the SS would withdraw westwards, but liquidate all prisoners first. That was no mere
suspicion on our part, subsequently we found out that Höss had
asked the camp commandant's office, on Himmler's behalf, what
measures would be necessary to level Birkenau to the ground and
erase every human trace. In our opinion this plan could only be
foiled by a joint operation with the Polish partisans. We had no

other choice but to move the leadership of the combat group outside the camp.

In the first few weeks Rudi was desperately unhappy. But then my friend Sari, who also worked in the registry office, fell head over heels in love with him. That's not so surprising, when one remembers that even the SS right up to the camp commandant had succumbed to his charm. I think there was another reason for Sari falling in love, which did not have so much to do with Rudi's appearance at all or with his reputation as a heart-breaker: In all those years we had stored up so much useless love, and thanks to the wedding it was set free and directed at the bridegroom. At first Rudi resisted, I noticed that he avoided Sari, stood back when she was busy anywhere near him, and avoided returning her glances as much as possible. He was even a little wooden or cold, which didn't deter my friend in the least; on the contrary, she only had eyes for him. He couldn't evade her approaches indefinitely, and finally the affection was mutual. Rudi soon found a good excuse to come regularly to our office. He explained to Kristan that out of gratitude to the registry office he had organised a bucket of oil. So now every Saturday afternoon he came to the hut with a big can, in order to rub the rough wooden floor. The time of day was a good one, because our superiors – apart from one guard – were off duty. Nevertheless, there was seldom the opportunity to become close, to exchange endearments. Now and again Rudi was able to give my friend a kiss behind a door or in the corner next to a cupboard. We office girls did everything we could to help make them happy. In confidence Sari showed me the love poems he wrote for her, and passed on to us all the information about military and political events which he supplied her with.

So the matter was settled: Ernst Burger and I would break out. Together with Zbyszek Raynoch, who worked with me in the SS precinct. We had to have someone with us who spoke Polish, otherwise our chances outside would have been minimal. Through civilian workers we got precise details about the escape route, the first shelter, food and making contact with the partisans. We found out when and where SS and police would search more intensively for us. In the infirmary we got hold of painkilling drugs and ones to strengthen the cirulatory system. Also poison capsules, in case our plan should fail. The problem was, we couldn't even tell our closest friends. They would be caught unprepared by our flight. Our families too could face reprisals. At best, we could cautiously prepare them for it in letters smuggled out of the camp. And then there was the question, who should move up into the leadership of the combat group after us.

Friemel, I said. I felt uneasy about the other Austrian we were thinking about. I wouldn't have doubted his courage. He took a lot of risks. But as kapo of the clothes store he lived in the lap of luxury. He had his own room, which was crammed full of linen and underwear. Once I knocked at his door, and he was just sitting down to supper with the roll call clerk and being served by two young prisoners. The table was literally groaning under all the delicacies: roast meat, vegetables, cake, alcohol, everything one could ever want. Come here, he said to me, hold out your cap. I was outraged by his magnanimity.

No, not him. Rudi.

Agreed, said Ernst Burger. I'll talk to him.

Two days before the planned escape Friemel came to see me.

I wanted to have a word with you, he said, because you already know me from Spain. I am well aware of the responsibility I'm taking on. To be honest, I don't feel good about it. There were times in the past when I did things that weren't quite right.

Don't talk nonsense. We know your work here in the camp. We trust you. There's no one better.

He said nothing for a while and stared at his shoes. Then he raised his head. He looked at me, but it was as if he was looking right through me.

I'm glad to hear that, he said, before you go.

It wasn't like that. He's forgetting one small detail. Because I already escaped before that. And before me Alfred Klahr, at my instigation. We were the only non-Poles who succeeded in escaping from the main camp. Klahr was shot two or three weeks later in Warsaw by a German patrol, apparently during a raid, just before the Uprising. That still leaves me. But he's simply put that out of his mind. A little while ago I heard him say on the radio, in front of a school class, that not a single Austrian succeeded in escaping from Auschwitz. Not long after I meet him in the street, take it up with him: Why do you say shit like that? Didn't I escape, am I a ghost or something? To which he replied: Sure, except you're a Yid. That dumb reply just about made me explode, but my doctor has told me I must never get excited. I would have loved to have settled the matter there and then. Let our fists do the talking, my dear Hermann. But what does that look like, two old fogeys, beating each other's brains out in the street.

Back to Klahr. He was the comrade who was sitting in the broom cupboard of Block 4 and in tiny, almost illegible writing composing his treatise on the national question. Friemel then sent it to Vienna, with an SS man, a Karl Hölblinger, who was evidently a good guy. He regularly brought old Friemel post, supposedly he even looked him up at work, at Brown Boveri, where Friemel senior was working as porter. Well, Klahr. Our German brothers couldn't be persuaded that Austria wasn't part of their beat. As a result even in Auschwitz there were ugly arguments, among the prisoners! It's no coincidence, after all, that Klahr writes the KPD (German Communist Party) has ended up floating in the wake of the Nazis. OK, and I refused to escape, before Alfred Klahr had escaped. He was our great theorist, teacher at the Lenin School in Moscow, tried and tested in the underground struggle, a man who had made a great contribution. I forced the matter through with considerable difficulty. Today I wonder, what did I get him into, if he had stayed in Auschwitz, he might still be alive. But as it was, he died.

My case was different. I was due to be liquidated on the instruction of the Vienna Gestapo. That's why Ernst Burger gave me priority. I got away on 22nd July with the Pole Szymon Zaydow. Everything was all right during the escape, we then separated, he went to Krakow, but the fact that he was a Jew almost cost him his life. Not because of the Nazis, his own countrymen let him down. Their damned anti-semitism. We met twice after the war, in the Polish People's Republic, that was something special to me, I envied him, being allowed to participate in building socialism, but he was sceptical, at our last meeting already quite demoralised, of course, he knew the reality there, and I, like a complete idiot, acted the super-Stalinist. In 1956 he emigrated to Australia, I wrote to him a couple of times, he didn't reply.

But I'm running ahead. We had got to July1944, midsummer. I was already long gone. And the head of the group is still in the camp.

The flirtation went on like that for two months, until I noticed that my friend was very nervous. She was weeping all the time, and her hands were trembling. I took her to task, and then she confided in me that Rudi was firmly determined to escape with a couple of comrades. And he absolutely wanted to take her with him. But she was afraid, she couldn't make up her mind right away and asked for a few days to think about it. Rudi kept on at her: either right away or not at all. You know what they're going to do with you, when the camp is cleared. On top of that our organisation has been uncovered. It's only a matter of hours, at most days, before they have us all. Sari hesitated. Then it was too late.

It may be that the wedding had all kinds of effects, psychologically, I mean. But the recognition that things were getting urgent, didn't come till the end of July. One day there was a small crowd outside the gate, figures, their feet bloody from walking, in rags, hollow-cheeked, terribly sick, they could hardly stand. That was what the Nazis had left over of Maidanek. All the other prisoners there had been liquidated on the spot or had died during the forced march. It was suddenly clear to us that we had to act. So that Auschwitz doesn't end in the same way. To bring about an uprising from outside or at least to organise armed resistance. Or should I put it cynically: to get the Party cadres to safety in time. Because they'll be needed, the political prisoners, after the end of Nazi rule, when it comes to the struggle for noble Socialism. Although at the time we were not at all agreed how things would go on in Europe. I remember, that around this time Friemel made an analysis, which someone was able to smuggle out of the camp. In it he put down reflections on the postwar order. He thought it quite possible that the Western Allies could still ally themselves to a Nazi Germany (without Hitler, that at least). He wasn't so far wrong. If we say: post-Nazi Germany, then his prediction is right. Someone who could figure all that out on the basis of wireless broadcasts, there in his work detail, was no fool. We discussed it. Heated interventions about the right strategy, political alliances, division of spheres of influence. Nonsense, shit, wise guys. Right there the Jews were being exterminated. One way or another that mass murder wasn't part of our political calculations.

So two days beforehand he says to me: I'm glad to hear that before you go. Two days later we're still there. Because we've got news that the partisans who were waiting for us outside have been attacked. Communication has broken off. The escape has to be postponed.

And when it's ready to start, I've long ago been moved to another camp, hundreds of miles to the northwest.

The original idea was not bad: Wearing a stolen SS uniform and with a forged pass I was supposed to escort the detainees Burger and Raynoch out of the camp. We would then have hidden in the elevator shaft of a former grain silo within the outer cordon, which was drawn up during the day. As a rule this sentry line was maintained for three nights after an escape. We would have tried to make our way to the first shelter on the fourth night.

The new plan, but I only discovered that later, diverged from the old one in every respect. First of all, there was no prisoner willing and able to escape who, like me, could play the part of an

SS man, second, it could be assumed that this time the outer cordon would be maintained for longer than three nights. How long couldn't be predicted. But because of that there was no possibility of an escape in two stages, using an interim hiding place in the camp area. So it was hard to know what to do. And this is where Rudi Friemel becomes involved again.

And it was he who organised the escape. He persuaded an SS man, a driver, to take part. This man was to drive out of the camp in a truck, with crates, and hidden in the crates would be Ernst Burger and a Pole and – I think there were three of them. And this SS man, Frank he was called, told a second SS man, a Sudeten German, who said, he'll join in too. He was very active in the preparations for the escape.

The 27th October at 10 in the morning was set as the time. The meeting point is in front of the clothes store. The trucks leave from there with the dirty washing. One of the escapees, the Pole Edek, still has to take a note to the SS kitchen beforehand. That's his task every day, he can't give it a miss today of all days and jeopardise the escape. So he goes to the kitchen and waits for the SS man, to whom he's supposed to hand the message. Quarter to ten and still no sign of him. Ten to ten. Edek grows uneasy. At six minutes to ten he puts the note on the German's desk, then he runs over to the clothes store barrack. It's just after ten when he gets there. No sign of his comrades. Could they already have hidden themselves on one of the trucks? He has forgotten the licence number of the escape vehicle, and he doesn't know either, which of the drivers is the right one. He stands there uncertainly and watches as the trucks drive off one after the other. Edek is disappointed. So they didn't wait for him, those few minutes. His shoulders drooping, he returns to his work party. In one hour, at most two, the escape will be discovered, then the alarm siren will wail, then SS men with tracker dogs will search the camp, then the Political Section will order all those suspected of helping the escape to be shut up in the bunker.

But nothing happens, Edek. No siren to be heard. Your friends must already have got some way.

Suddenly the door of the orderly room is flung open. A runner bursts in. He gasps the names of the escapees: Ernst, Zbyszek, Benek, Piotr, Czesiek, who at the last moment stood in for Edek. The runner reported, staccato, he is still out of breath. The latest news. Edek listens. One cannot say that he feels as if new-born.

The SS man, whom Friemel recruited, was supposed to drive a truck to Bielsko, to the laundry. But no, he wanted to escape too, so it was the other one, the Sudeten German, Johann Roth, who was at the wheel, and Frank was hidden in a chest at the back like the prisoners. Roth would then have let them out on the way. That's how it was planned. But Roth betrayed everything to the Gestapo. Who is in the chests and where the partisans are waiting for them, that is, in the village inn at Leki. The truck really did drive off and was stopped at the checkpoint. Several armed SS men got on, the vehicle turned round and drove up to Block 11. The escapees were hauled out of the chests. I assume they had already realised that the escape had failed, and taken poison. The doctors immediately undertook a partial gastrectomy. Zbyszek and Czesiek died nevertheless. The SS had meanwhile sur-

rounded the inn at Leki, there was a gun battle, in which two partisans were killed and three captured. And immediately after that
they also took away Friemel, because Roth, who betrayed the
attempt, stated that he and Vesely had planned the whole action.
That they had acquired false passes and made contact with the
partisans. So Friemel and Vesely were caught too. I've never heard
before that they were also going to escape. The only way I can
make sense of it is that their escape was to take place at a later
point. Then almost the whole of the underground command
would have been outside. It's just like Friemel that he absolutely
wanted to have his girlfriend with him. Vesely was likewise head
over heels in love, with Jolana, a Jewess from Slovakia, whom he
had met in Birkenau. Presumably he wanted to take her as well.
Two pairs of lovers, how romantic. Irresponsible, if you ask me.
Fighting or cuddling. You can't do both. I don't want to pass
judgement on Friemel, but it was criminal stupidity to trust an SS
man. And why did he want to get away? In all likelihood nothing
would have happened to him in Auschwitz. He had the best hand
of all of us: He counted as a Reich German, he was well-fed,
strong, motivated, part of the camp structure, he had good con-
tacts up to the very top. The girl in the registry office? Yes, it could
have ended badly for her.

Rudi had already had a premonition that it would turn out badly.
An SS man had caved in at the last minute, we heard that, and also
that Rudi was accused of having, over time, smuggled out food,
clothing, cards and medicines. But worst, of course, were the
escape attempt and the contact with the partisans. Rudi was
brought to our section more than once for interrogation. He was
tortured in the room next door, we knew it, but through the thin

walls we heard neither the blows nor the panting of those dealing out the blows, nor Rudi's cries of pain. Or do I only imagine it. Am I in a film, which never stops, which goes on running soundlessly: Rudi, Sari, the death certificates in front of me and the book of the dead and the letters from Switzerland, from my son, whom one day I will see again on the border bridge at Sankt Margrethen.

Usually the SS took their time. Often Rudi had to wait six or eight hours for interrogation. That was particularly hard for Sari. Out of fear of giving herself away, she didn't dare show him even the least sign of affection. She cowered at her desk, staring down, her face drained of blood. Now and then I managed to give Rudi or one of his fellow-sufferers a glass of water without being seen.

The five of them defended themselves very cleverly. So despite the incriminating evidence their guilt could not be proven beyond doubt. Apart from that an unanticipated struggle erupted over them between the head of the Political Section and Baer, the commandant of the main camp. Brose, the head of the Gestapo in Kattowitz, called on Baer in order to plead for the accused. He said, one should take into account, that Rudi was a privileged prisoner and his marriage in the camp was useful propaganda as a humanitarian gesture. Even Hössler, the prisoners' commandant, was against execution. However, Baer had promoted SS man Roth for revealing the plot, and so it was a question of his prestige. He would have regarded a pardon as a personal defeat.

So everyone was waiting for the sentence. Again and again our thoughts wandered to Block 11, where the bunker was.

His real name was Jakob Kozelczuk, but everyone just called him Bunker Jakob. He was the trusty, he had to make sure the prisoners were capable of being interrogated or undress them before they were shot. In the camp there was a rumour he had been the trainer of Max Schmeling, the world boxing champion, Schmeling once later denied it. But he could have been, no doubt about it. A giant of a man, with the paws and the strength of a bear, who spoke a curious mixture of Polish, German, Yiddish, Russian and English. Despite his dreadful job, he was quite well-liked. After the war he emigrated to Israel, where he got by as a showman and strongman. Legal proceedings against him were dropped thanks to exonerating testimony in his defence. He knew how to make the beatings he had to administer at once terrifying and considerate. Someone claimed Jakob helped his co-religionists, that is, Jews, above all. He had been less generous to all others. But that's not true. For example, he twice saved my life. The first time, when at the command of a member of the Political Section, he searched me and deliberately overlooked the note in my breast pocket with the names of Jewish prisoners. If he had shown it to the SS man, it would have been over for all of us. The second time when, during a Bunker selection, he stood me in a dark corner, so that Grabner didn't notice me. Jakob was often enough in the Bunker himself because of his generous escapades. Because he was caught handing out cigarettes, medicines and blankets, because he warned us about informers, because he gave food to prisoners in the standing cells, because he passed on news of accomplices. On several occasions he also had to stand in as hangman. At one of these executions, the rope broke. Jakob thought the SS would grant the man his life, as apparently was the custom in the Middle Ages. But the victim was hanged a second time. And this time Jakob was condemned to the Bunker for a very long time, he was close to being strung up himself. But he was too useful to the SS for that. Since he had access to all stores they could get hold of anything through him.

Jakob. Jakob Kozelczuk. And Rudi Friemel, Burger, Vesely, the two Poles. I can well imagine, that he disobeyed orders and immediately gave them an opportunity to confer. So they were able to co-ordinate their statements. It's known that all five sent messages out via Bunker Jakob, not only to the members of the combat group. I suspect it was again Hölblinger who took their letters to Vienna. At least one letter from Vesely reached his mother and another his girlfriend in Birkenau. In the latter he thanks her for the warm socks and the jumper, which she had smuggled into the bunker for him. Without Jakob it would not have been possible.

Our furtive glances, across to the Bunker, across to the Appelplatz. That's where the gallows is constructed, where it's dismantled and removed, when the instruction comes from Berlin to defer the sentence for the time being and to continue the investigations. It's set up a second time, taken down again. Powerful hammer blows, silent in my head. This stillness all around, this wordlessness, this listening and waiting for something that doesn't come, this silence which tears the silence in two.

4

NINETY PER CENT

28/10/44 – Dearest Marga, my fears have come true: I'm in the bunker. I do not know if these lines will ever reach you; I'm writing to you nevertheless, in these hours it is a tremendous relief for me. I hope everything turns out well! Yesterday some comrades tried to escape. They were caught because a soldier betrayed them. Immediately afterwards Ludwig and I were also detained. We already have one terrible interrogation behind us. If they go on like this, I shall have to kill myself. There are two dead so far.

1/11 – Today they continued with the interrogation, this time it wasn't quite as bad. Ludwig is out of danger. They didn't beat him very badly. I think it looks a little better, but it's still uncertain whether I will survive. There are already three dead. This afternoon they imprisoned us in one cell, there are still five of us left.

5/11 – We've found out that the investigations have been concluded, now they're sending the file to Berlin. We made a good impression during the interrogations because of our steady bearing. No one has said anything bad about anyone else, everyone takes the blame on himself. Nevertheless the situation is a bit dubious. I know that. We have to expect an extremely harsh sentence. Shooting or hanging. As soon as there's news I'll go on writing.

12/12 – We're still alive. They say the business will turn out well. The camp commandant will intervene on our behalf. A comfort, because our fate now depends on Berlin. The others here are antici-pating the death sentence. There are three of us from Vienna and two Poles. Ludwig will get away with it and send you these lines. He is not badly incriminated, but Ernst and I are known as 'incorrigible Reds', and the others are just Poles.

20/11 – Poor little woman, it is time to say some very serious words to you. Today they told us that the file has come back from Berlin. In short, they say: 'You have to be prepared for the worst.' That means they're going to execute us.

In the last few days I've thought about my life. When one's expect-ing the end, one looks deep into oneself. I can recognise my failings and the weaknesses of my character without false sentimentality. I became familiar with women very early – at sixteen. When love was only beginning for others, I already knew almost everything about their good and ugly sides. I took women as they came, and didn't think that highly of them. There was never a tragedy, but nor did I ever feel what people call true love. It went on like that for years. Only in prison did I resolve to give up these fleeting relationships and devote myself entirely to my work and the political struggle. And it wasn't difficult for me to put this decision into practice.

Until you came along. In you I saw the woman to whom I can give my heart and for the first time I felt what love is, not just sexual desire.

But we were never able to lead a normal life. In addition to the circumstances we know all too well, there were the bad sides of my character, the remnant of the life, that I had left behind me. So we didn't really find a way to each other. Your great vulnerability as well as your emotional and physical exhaustion in the fight for our survival made the inner distance even greater. And the enforced separation threatened to tear us apart for ever.

In the meantime it had become clear to me how much you mean to me. But you also found your way to me. After your experiences with other men you took the same path as I did: towards a life together. These experiences hit me very hard, but through them I have also gained a family: my wife and my child. Even if I did not yet have your love, I was nevertheless tremendously happy. Now I was able to have a proper idea of our child and his future; I was able to regard you as my true wife. And you have come to the same conclusion, your letter, which I received the day before my arrest, tells me that. Worried and anxious, I followed the news of the air raids on Vienna. But I always had the hope of seeing you and our little son again one day.

Life here has gone on, the struggle too. I could not stop fighting, you understand that. And now fate has caught up with me, as it already has with millions of others. Here and in this way my life ends.

I am not sad, and you should not be either, Marga. I have done my duty. I die head held high and for my ideals. What's painful is to have the end of the human path of suffering in sight, without still being able to help, without being able to help in building a new world, without being able to enjoy with you the fruits of such great sacrifice.

When the war is over, you will return to Spain, my second homeland, which I love above all others. Take care of our son, bring him up to be a human being who is there for other human beings. Try to find a solution for yourself, which allows you to forget how terrible it was to live with me. Forgive me for everything, that I have done to you.

Then I can depart easily.

I shall think of you and Edi until the very last moment. I embrace you both and kiss you,

Your Rudi.

1/12 – Dearest, so far I know nothing certain about our fate. Dreadful, this uncertainty. Of course, we hope to escape the worst, and perhaps we'll be lucky, even if the chances are very small. Strictly speaking the situation is not so bad at all: The war could even be over this year. 'Could', I say, it is more likely that it will last until February or March.

Christmas is just around the corner. You will be alone with my beloved boy. Next year you will already be celebrating Christmas with your brother and sister or with me, if the business here ends well. Don't be cross with me, if I don't write to you in the next few days. You can understand that I don't feel calm enough to do so. At this moment I want to remain tough, and sentimental thoughts make me weak. With all my heart and love I wish you both the very best, peace and happiness. Above all I wish that you both come through the air raids unharmed, that is my greatest worry now.

It would be better if you only write me normal letters now. Tomorrow or the day after I will try to send this one off, it will perhaps no longer be possible later on. Don't send me any parcels, not for Christmas either. Instead, please send me a letter or a card every week, so that I know how you both are.

Father will write to the camp commandant, to ask him if I am still alive. You do so too. Promise?

3/12 – Dear poor Marga. The file has come back, because it was not complete. That means we will be interrogated again. That isn't bad news, on the contrary, it means that so far the request for the death penalty has not been granted. The struggle for our lives goes on. It will last weeks yet, and time is life.

Marga, perhaps you are angry with me, because I have written all of that to you. But there are two reasons: first, you should know everything about my life and suffering in these crucial days, so that you can be strong, if one day a letter with a black border arrives. Second, it is a huge relief to me to be able to pour out my heart. (Tomorrow I shall try to send off this letter, I hope it will reach you.) Marga. I would like to weep into your hands to get rid of this great weariness, which I already feel. I am not afraid, you know me well enough to believe me when I say that. But it's all going on so long now. And I want to clasp you in my arms for ever at last. If I survive, I will do everything to see you again soon. I wonder what you're thinking of now, dearest.

7/12 – Our situation is a bit better today. Wait and see what happens. One thing is certain: I'll live to see Christmas, so you must promise me that on that day you'll spare a thought for your pest. – I embrace you with infinite longing, Your R.

Kiss my handsome boy for me!

14/12 – Dearest Marga, I couldn't send the letter on the 8th, but I'll manage it tomorrow.

There's good news. Unless there are complications to come, they won't execute us. We are 90% saved. If they don't kill us, we'll get 25 strokes on the backside – perhaps 50 – and be released from the bunker. They'll probably transfer us to another camp. Would that not be wonderful? In two to three weeks we'll know more. Until then everything will remain unclear. Let us hope for the best!

Ludwig is already entirely out of danger. He'll get out of the bunker soon. You must tell his mother that, and emphasise it, so that she really *believes it. Give her greetings from him, he wishes her all the best for Christmas and the New Year. She shouldn't worry, her baby is doing all right, as incidentally are the others.*

Ernst is in the same position as I am. It's important that his sister is told all that. But neither she nor Frau Vesely should say a single word about it in their letters to the two of them.

Perhaps in a while you can write to me in Spanish again, but then you must hand over your letter immediately when you receive my next one.

Well then, now I can dream of our reunion after all. Oh girl, how much I long for it! Will you still be mine then? Think a little of me, dear woman, don't forget me altogether. It's terrible not to have any news from you. Up until now I haven't received any normal letters either. Are you not writing to me any more?

My dear, dear Marga, I embrace you passionately and wish you all the best for Christmas.

Always

Your R.

What is my little headstrong boy up to? Write me a lot about him, girl. A great big kiss for both of you!

5

THE SCAR

It's very hard, to have someone like you as father. What can I say? Of course I have tried to measure myself against you. But ultimately I didn't know much about you. Nothing at all really. Nor did I try to find out more about you, about your life, because you were a hero, and in that war there were many heroes no one talked about. To me you were one more, one to whom I happened to be related, and what could I have done, to hold my own with him. It's better if I don't talk about myself at all, and if I do, then only out of courtesy to you: I studied psychology, I'm a lecturer in statistics, at a university, I'm married, my wife is a doctor, a specialist in sports medicine, we have two children, we're already grandparents. We have a house outside Paris, we have a holiday home on Minorca, we probably also have a car and a dog. We have no police record and are creditworthy. My wife's name is Françoise. Her father was executed during the German occupation. The Gestapo raided the printer's, where he was producing *L'Humanité* and other illegal works. That's not important. I only said it just now, so that you can feel satisfied. But it's true. Our daughter Laura is in her early thirties, has two children, she works in an advice centre for unemployed young people, I think her marriage is a happy one. Our son is still single, he's an energy technologist, an engineer, he's writing his thesis, in his spare time he builds energy-saving bicycles, each one more eccentric than the last. Instead of doing military service he was a voluntary worker in Cameroon. Incidentally, he bears your name: Rodolphe. I wanted to please my mother.

Ask him whether he remembers me. He must be able to remember.

    – It's long ago. He was too young.

    – He cannot have forgotten me.

    – He was a three-year-old child.

    – He was there. He bounced on my knee. Humpty-Dumpty sat on a wall, Humpty-Dumpty had a great fall. He shouted out loud with happiness. Again! Everyone heard us.

    – That was years ago, decades. Look at him, he's got grey hair.

    – Look at me. I haven't changed. Nothing is past. He must remember.

    – He says, the train journey.

    – Yes, yes, the compartment. And what else?

    – The soot, he says. All the songs. Then, when the journey never seemed to end.

    – What else? He has to remember.

I don't know when I heard about it. Sometime in 1945, I think. My mother heard about it. From my grandfather, I imagine. I was thirteen then, but I don't remember anything more about the circumstances. I've found a letter, also from 1945, in it my grandfather is still writing to the camp commandant, he's anxious, because he hasn't heard from his son for a long time. There was already something underway about people being released, and they promised him, if the Russians advance any further, then the execution won't happen. Then he's got a good chance. That's apparently what they said to my grandfather. Later I found out more. I thought, if there had been more people like him, then we would have been spared a lot. That was my feeling. Only I'm not certain if I myself would have been one of them. Although I would like to have been committed in that way, or would want to be. But would I have acted as he did, despite a family? Perhaps the family would have gone along with it, and the result would have been much the same. But perhaps not. But otherwise − I can't say that he did something wrong. I would never hold his determination against him. He's an example to me.

I remember the train journey. It's not my first memory. I associate the first with the image of my grandfather in Vienna: I'm sitting on the kitchen chair and I'm putting a piece of bread in my mouth. It's hard, and I have to chew vigorously. Suddenly my grandfather is standing in front of me, small and thin, an empty fold of skin hanging over his buttoned-up shirt collar. He looks angry, he's shaking me, because I ate his bread.

My second memory, that's my mother's wide-open mouth. She's kneeling on the floor in front of me and trying to teach me the days of the week in German. She speaks loudly and clearly, with exaggerated facial expressions. I have to laugh.

In my third memory I'm running home from kindergarten. I

want to surprise my mother. I open the door, stretch out my arm and shout: Heil Hitler! I see my mother's narrow frame buckling as if struck by a whip.

My fourth memory, the wailing of the sirens before an air raid.

My fifth memory, a feeling that blots out all perceptions: fear.

My sixth memory, the hum of a bomber squadron, distant explosions, the rattling of the windowpanes.

My seventh memory, as every other time I'm going down to the air raid shelter with a little black case. I'm already at the cellar door. There's a crash, the stairwell collapses into rubble. My mother jumps down to me in the middle of a thick cloud of dust.

In my tenth or eleventh memory I'm lying in a hospital ward. Another boy, in the bed next to me, steals the biscuits my mother has brought. Once I see her standing in the doorway, at the other end of the ward, the red beret on her dark hair, and I'm shouting for her and crying and thrashing about, and she's crying too, as she's pushed out by two nurses, because she's come too late, it's not visiting time.

A memory in between, which I'm unable to place: My mother is kneeling or standing on the windowsill, the window is wide open, it looks as if she is about to throw herself out of the window. Someone or something holds her back.

A late memory, dead people in the street.

Even later, Soviet soldiers, they give me a piece of chocolate.

Then the last memory before the memory of the train journey: Schloss Wilheminenberg on the edge of the Vienna Woods, high above the city. Thick walls, high rooms, plaster orna-mentation, brass fittings, smell of camphor, wards. The corridors are also obstructed by beds. There are many Spaniards, they laugh and sing. One says, I should raise my arm and clench my fist.

And then? What happened then?

    – Then came the long train journey, he says.

    – That can't be right. That was before. He must mean the journey to Germany. Or the one to Vienna. Or from Vienna to Auschwitz, to our wedding.

    – The journey from Vienna.

    – To Spain? So I was right. I was sure that Marga would return to her country.

    – Not to Spain, to France. With this man. Paco.

    – Her brother Paco? Did he come to fetch her?

    – Not Paco Ferrer. Paco Suárez.

    – …

    – Are you jealous?

    – I'm asking the questions here. He should just answer my questions. I want to know who Suárez is.

Margarita and Suárez got to know each other in Vienna. At the end of the war my sister had lost a lot of weight and was very weak. So she was sent to a sanatorium. And there were Spanish Republicans there, who had survived Mauthausen, Suárez was one of them. Was it love? Probably the feeling of being alone. Margarita always needed someone to protect her. I only saw her again years later, her and my nephew Edi and my brother Paco, who stayed in France after the war and taught Spanish and Latin in a nuns' school. They didn't know that I was imprisoned for five years. I didn't get a passport until 1954. And Paco and Marga invited me to Paris, they paid for the trip, I didn't have one measly duro to spare, how could I have. As a Red I couldn't get any work, least of all as a teacher, I gave private tuition for next to nothing. Fernando, of course, had also lost his job at the bank. He got by as a sales rep, of corks for bottles. Hard-earned money. Later he managed to travel in goods with better profit margins, lace, square scarves, linen, surgical instruments. He had to drive all round Spain. In 1953 he at last got a job where he didn't have to travel, as bookkeeper in a publishing house that specialised in modern music. Sheet music and so on. And fourteen years later he began to set up the League of Disabled and War Invalids of the Republic.

So in 1954 I went to Paris and saw my brother and sister again and told them what had happened to me in the meantime. I still remember very well, the political officer of their Party cell had warned them about me: Be careful with her, she's coming from the Fascist zone! Perhaps she's an informer. Says someone, who has never known what it's like to breathe prison air. But that was the atmosphere in those days, fear and distrust everywhere.

I felt uneasy about Suárez the moment I set eyes on him. Yet fundamentally he wasn't a bad person. He was odd, uncommunicative and half crazy, to be honest. He was an illegitimate child. His mother was from León. But he was born in Madrid, in Carabanchel. He grew up with an uncle, who often hit him. I think that the childhood and the years in the concentration camp marked him for ever. He was terribly young when the Germans picked him up and carried him off to Mauthausen. I don't want to know everything he went through there. He never talked about it either, not a word. They must have brainwashed him, he was traumatised, he was embittered, but that's no reason to make life difficult for the boy and my sister. All day long commands rained down. Order was the highest virtue. For years they had to sit on boxes, because he thought chairs an unnecessary luxury, for years drink their breakfast coffee out of tin cans. I was imprisoned longer than he was, but I would never even have dreamt of making do with the wretched jail conditions. On the day I was released, the first thing I did was drink coffee out of a proper cup.

Being with them was like being in prison. And Marga accepted it all without a murmur, I was just itching to give her a slap, because she was agreeing with everything. It made me feel ill just to watch. I stayed with them for four days, after all, I loved my sister very much, but that was enough; I knew, either I'm going to scratch this man Suárez's face or I'm leaving. Perhaps she was quite happy with him, she had always been like that, avoided making any decisions. Although she certainly had a mind of her own, she let him have his way, out of convenience or who knows why. My poor nephew. He was thirteen then. And it hurt me to see how they bossed him around. Edi, do this, Edi, don't do that, Edi, you must be home at seven on the dot! Unbearable.

Vienna–Paris, I remember that. It was a long journey, two or three days or more, the train often stopped between stations. At the beginning it was a great adventure for me, the compartment was crowded, only Spaniards, cheerful, they sang folk songs, revolutionary songs, songs from the Civil War. Gradually the euphoria gave way to exhaustion. I began to believe we would never arrive. We had black faces from the soot, from the locomotive.

That was in autumn 1945.

The French authorities billeted us in Montrouge, a suburb in the south of the city, in an old tumble-down house. The three of us got one small room. There was a big double bed. There must have been a second bed, for me, but I only remember the big bed in the small room. There was also a kitchen, several kitchens. I remember that the men went out to look for work. Gradually they all found something. I remember that the women peeled potatoes together. I remember the children, nearly all of them were older than me. My stepfather Paco has told me that we couldn't understand each other because I could only speak German. That one day I was crying and he asked me, why was I laughing, because he didn't know the word for crying, and each time he asked I became even more angry and cried all the more. I don't remember that. I only know that in Montrouge I very quickly learned Spanish. And that there I became a bed-wetter. That Paco punished me for it, he forced me to stand for hours with my arms in the air. I didn't dare lower them, even when he wasn't in the room. I also remember that.

After a couple of weeks we moved to Cachan, not far from Montrouge. The owner of a dilapidated pavilion had to give up two rooms on the ground floor for us. The building stood in an overgrown park with magnificent trees, limes and chestnuts, and there were also lilacs and roses. We lived in Cachan until the mid-'50s.

Paco was a metalworker. His company was in the north of Paris. So he had a long way to work, right across the city, had to change more than once, it took him two hours each way. I never saw him before eight in the evening. My mother also worked, all her life. She painted neon signs, with gold dust, toxic paints. She also worked for a furrier and in a dye works. At Flaminaire she filled gas cigarette lighters. Finally she was a cleaner.

In the evening they were both often out, at Party meetings, courses or lectures, and I had to remain at home alone. In Cachan there were lots of rats. I was frightened of them, and when I couldn't fall asleep because I was afraid, I began to sing to myself, my mother's lullabies. I liked them better than the fighting songs from the Civil War, which Paco had neatly written out in an exercise book.

At five I started infant school. There I was forced to learn French. Presumably after a year I still spoke with an accent or now and again used a German word, at any rate, at school I was beaten up more than once. *Boche,* the other boys called me. *Sale boche.*

Cachan was a poor district. Nevertheless, every child at school had a couple of crayons and also a proper fountain pen, while I had to make do with a pencil. When I lost it one day, I had nothing to write with, because my mother couldn't buy me a new one right away. As punishment I had to stand in the corner. But in general I didn't notice many differences between myself and the other pupils.

That only changed when I started at the Lycée Louis Le Grand, an elite school in the centre of Paris, where the bourgeoisie sent their children. I felt rather lost there. My parents had enrolled me because my primary school teacher had advised them to do so, I was very hard-working and talented, they should try it. And I passed the entrance exam. In those days the school had a good reputation.

So at the age of eleven I realised that people are not equal. First of all, my new fellow-pupils were better dressed. Second, they talked about things I knew nothing about, cruises, seaside resorts, servants. Third, they could afford school books, school bags, fountain pens, protractors. I, on the other hand, never had a Latin dictionary. It was far too expensive, so I always used the dictionaries of my schoolmates. Altogether I bought as few books as possible. And I was also very economical with paper. That's stayed with me till today; I'm still reluctant to use blank sheets of paper. I always reach for paper that's been written on. I've never suffered from this lack, on the contrary, it made me more balanced.

What did bother me, though, at seventeen and eighteen, was that I didn't have a homeland. I never felt myself to be Spanish, because the noise, the loudness, the gregariousness are alien to me. I'm too discreet, too restrained for that. And I had quite a lot of aversion to everything French. After all, I saw how shabbily the people here behave to foreigners. The Spaniards as well, at least in the beginning. They're too lazy to learn the language, people said. Even after ten years, my mother had to let herself be humiliated at the baker on the corner if she wanted to buy a baguette. The salesgirls acted dumb. They pretended they couldn't understand the woman. We weren't integrated. We had no French friends. Not one. I can't remember how many times I heard that we should finally clear off. That we were living at their expense. I also saw how they treated the people from the colonies. That's why I was never proud to be French. I said to myself, ok, I just don't have a homeland, I only have a fatherland: Austria. When I was eighteen I went to the consulate, so that I could at last get a passport. Impossible, they said. I then presented them with two dozen documents, and they had to grant me Austrian citizenship whether they liked it or not. At twenty-one I became French nevertheless. I could prove that I had been living in the country for more than ten years. But it didn't make me happy.

It may be true that the Spanish largely stuck together. They were living as if they were on standby. They were convinced that Franco wouldn't last long, and then they wanted to go back to their country. They drank to it at New Year: Next year in Spain! That hope held up until the middle of the '50s. At some point they stopped drinking to it.

It was wonderful to see them again, nevertheless. We laughed a lot, the two of us, as we told each other sad stories from our lives. She said hardly anything about Rudi. Because the other man was always there. Paco, Paco Suárez. Only once did he go to a Party meeting in the evening. Then she brought out a folder, with photos and Rudi's letters, and I was able to read them at last. Margarita also talked about Rudi when we went shopping, but little, very little, because most of the time we weren't alone. Either the boy was there or this homebody Suárez, who never opened his mouth.

I was nine, when my mother told me about my father for the first time. It was at home, in the presence of my stepfather. I didn't take in much — that Rudi was a political commissar in the International Brigades, that he was then deported to Auschwitz, that there he took part in the resistance to the camp authorities. My mother described him as a great personality, as a man of extraordinary virtues. He was particularly likeable, he was always laughing, he didn't lose his sense of humour even in the most difficult situations. He had a very good character, said my mother. She maintained that I looked like him. The spitting image. She also showed me the poem he had written for me. I should fulfil my mother's every wish, not cause her any pain, stand up for myself, follow his path, fight for progress. What was I supposed to do with these commandments? No one taught me how one follows after a hero.

Go on!
    — You're tormenting him.
    — It's not me who's tormenting him. He is, he's tormenting

himself.

−What more do you want from him? You know almost everything.

− I don't know anything. He has to talk.

−What for? It's past.

− Nothing is past. He must help me by going on talking. I want to know if she forgot me.

−You were her great love, he says. That's why she so rarely talked about you. It would have been embarrassing for him, to ask her to say more about you. He didn't want to hurt her.

− Because of the other man? Because she was unhappy with him?

−Yes, because of Suárez.

Marga and Suárez weren't at all suited. I asked myself why she got involved with him at all. She was convinced she wouldn't cope on her own. How can I support myself and my child? Quite simply, by doing what you've been doing so far. Working. Aren't you slaving away eight or nine hours a day anyway? Well, there you are. Keep on slaving away and be there for the boy. Nobody interferes. Nobody bosses you around. You're independent. You manage wonderfully. But she evidently needed a man at her side. In that respect she was exactly like my mother, without a man in the house it was the end of the world for her. For me it was never a problem. But her: The boy needs a father. I guessed what would happen.

That they then got married nevertheless, was ultimately my fault. I was against it. But if something has to be, then I always want it to be clear-cut. And because I realised that that's what she was longing for, I hauled Suárez over the coals. I told him, I'm giving you two years. If you haven't married her by then, I'm coming back, and I'll chuck you out, and if you don't go of your own free will, I'll fetch my brother. I left two days later. And he promptly married her. She would never have dared ask him. She sent me the wedding photo. In her place I would have shown him the door. But she was convinced there has to be a man, a figure of authority. A single woman can't manage. Nonsense! He exploited her. I simply didn't understand her.

Later on, when she was ill, he really did look after her. One has to grant him that. He nursed her, self-sacrificingly. He was good at that. But otherwise.

In character my mother was typically Spanish: very emotional, very dramatic, very tragic. She often wept. She filled me with guilt feelings. At one time at the beginning of the '50s she had all the symptoms of a pregnancy; she wasn't pregnant at all, but she was nauseous, she put on weight, she would unexpectedly be overcome by a ravenous hunger for pickled cucumbers or hard-boiled eggs. In fact she couldn't have got pregnant by Paco anyway, my stepfather was infertile. He had headaches for days on end, suffered from depressions, perhaps because of Mauthausen. He was certainly well-liked by his workmates, he could be charming and obliging in company. But at home he often didn't say a word to us for a whole week. Once he slapped my face, my cheek was swollen for days. When I was already grown up, my mother asked me if she should get a divorce from him. I advised her against it. That was a mistake. But I felt sorry for him. Because he always had in his mind what had happened to his father, who had left wife and children and emigrated to France, where as an old man he lived in a miserable hole, poor and lonely. Paco was afraid that the same thing would happen to him. That's why I was against my mother leaving him. Apart from that I had been scared by her sister Marina, who once visited us. She was over-excitable, she always knew everything better, she got into a fight with every man. That made Paco appear the lesser evil.

I never saw him hit the boy. In that respect Suárez was all right. But perhaps it's actually better for a child to get a smack occasionally and then to be embraced and kissed, than constantly to get this correct treatment. Correct, but without love, without passion. Freedom was not on the agenda with Suárez. There was a set daily routine, it could under no circumstances be changed. In Cullera, for example, where they later had a holiday home, one had to go for a walk at five on the dot, in August, on the Mediterranean, in the scorching heat. At seven one had to be back. At half past eight the evening meal had to be on the table and at ten everyone had to crawl into bed. Or: Once we went on holiday together, to a camping site in Hendaye in the French Basque Country. One day my sister and I went across the border to San Sebastian. By the harbour we ate some prawns. Without asking him! He raged, in his own way: by saying not another word to us. He didn't even look at us. He kept my sister dangling for a whole month. Lucky for him that he wasn't married to me. I would have paid him back in kind. I would have said, whatever you can do, I can do at least as well. I wouldn't have said anything either. Then I would have carried his bed to the junk room with my own hands, here, I would have said, here you've got a nice place to sleep.

At fourteen I caught TB. The doctors were at a loss; they were unable to pin down any real reason for me getting the illness. Today I realise that it was an illness of letting go, of rebellion against the world of my parents, which was suffocating me. But I never consciously opposed them. Their political ideals have also become mine. To me it was always clear that one must continue the struggle, even if in the end one's on one's own, and possibly even with nothing to show.

Perhaps there already was something on my lungs before that. Because when I was eight, I was allowed to spend a summer in Norway, as part of a relief action for eighty Spanish refugee children. My host family, a couple called Land, lived on a farm beside a forest, the next property was far away. There was milk and butter and meat in abundance. I was allowed to drive the cattle onto the meadow and swim in a lake. There was a ski-jump nearby. And in the middle of the forest there was a hut in which Mrs Land spun thread into wool. I learned a couple of Norwegian sentences. I also learned to ride a bicycle on one of these big heavy bikes. One day they were very alarmed, because I wasn't back for supper, and they looked for me with a horse and cart. It was like a fairy tale, a wonderful hot summer that I spent there. The Lands, whose own children were already grown up, would have liked nothing better than to adopt me. They wrote to us for at least two years. My parents only replied once, and so the contact broke off.

I think it was because of my stepfather. Paco was a man who strikes up friendships easily and breaks them off again just as easily. I remember that we became ever more isolated, because little by little he had fallen out with all his acquaintances. My mother suffered because of it, he even stopped her meeting her friends in Paris. Don't return visits, don't answer letters, don't show any sign of life. Unfortunately I have become like that too.

In my grandfather's box I found a bundle of letters, including carbon copies, which went back and forward between Vienna and Paris. The earliest ones still bear the Allies' censorship stamp. Evidently he wanted to take over the guardianship of my half-brother, but his daughter-in-law said that wasn't necessary. At the beginning she still writes in German, in a kind of phonetic spelling, and Eduard scribbles a couple of sentences as well, then communication evidently breaks off for years, because once my grandfather complains that he has written every two months, but never received a reply.

The later letters from Paris, from my father's second wife and from my half-brother, are written in Spanish. My grandfather had an acquaintance, who was married to a Spanish woman, she translated the letters for him. There was discussion of a convalescent holiday for my half-brother in Zakopane, which my grandfather had applied for through the concentration camp association. I don't even know if it ever happened. The first time, the application was made too late, the next year the woman couldn't get a holiday at the scheduled time, on a third occasion Eduard had to swot for his leaving certificate. So many letters, so much effort, so much wasted affection. Once my father's second wife writes sadly that Edi doesn't want to speak German any more, because the boys there in France call him a Nazi, once she reports, full of pride, that he's working hard at school, once she confesses coyly that she's got quite fat, once she reveals that she's considering getting married again. My grandfather has nothing against that, he even encourages her. The correspondence is altogether warm on both sides. At some point it breaks off.

I was in Vienna when I was seventeen or eighteen. I was travelling all over Europe and took the opportunity to visit my grandfather. He had written that he was ill and would die soon, and he wanted to see me once more. Vienna seemed very bourgeois to me, stuffed full of statues, hidden behind façades. A bit like Geneva. I had imagined the city to be more beautiful, livelier. I remember a park, there was an orchestra playing there, I listened to it for a while. The restaurants weren't expensive, I could afford to eat in them, only you got the same thing everywhere, schnitzel.

In a photo which my grandfather sent us just after the war he was very fat. When I visited him in Vienna he was again as slim as I remembered him. He was wearing out the suits of his youth. We were hardly able to communicate, because I had forgotten German long before. I think he had a position in the city administration, he was a councillor or something like that. His wife told my fortune from cards. She said there would be two women in my life, a blonde one and a dark one.

I didn't meet my father's brother. No one else at all of the family. I wasn't much interested, because my mother had told me that she was not made welcome by Rudi's relations. I don't think I spent the night with my grandfather. Perhaps I was even only in Vienna for a day.

My mother never met my father's second wife. But I did, I saw her very briefly once at my grandfather's, after the war. I also saw my half-brother. When, I don't know. I don't even know when he was born. I don't have any memories of him at all. I think his mother had a lot of freckles, but I'm not certain. I think so. But I don't know.

I also went to Spain for the first time at the end of the '50s, with my mother. I thought it was also the first time for her since her flight. Only at her funeral would I discover, that she had already crossed the border illegally before, with propaganda against the Franco regime. So she was not after all as timid as she had seemed.

As I remember it the stay in Madrid turned into one non-stop party. I got to know my relatives. Everyone was in a good mood, open, carefree, there were people standing around or sitting everywhere in the apartment, everyone was talking at someone else. The district of Lavapiés, where my aunt was living at the time, was also full of life, the streets were crowded with people until late at night, they shouted, laughed, sang, clapped their hands, pushed each other forward. If they wanted to talk to each other, they came to a halt. That was something I noticed: that the Spanish have to come to a stop when they're having a conversation. Just as cockerels close their eyes when they're crowing.

When my boy and Margarita's boy were eighteen, we all went to Minorca. A cousin in Seville warned us, he said, as soon as the relations in Mahón see you, they'll bar the door. Because they had lots of money, but were very stingy. They were misers. Our grandfather, the pharmacist, had already passed away. A prominent man on the island, they posthumously awarded him an important order, the 'Alfonso X El Sabio'. Maybe he deserved it. But as a human being he was a disaster. Arrogant, with a violent temper and lacking any self-control. He used to hit his children with a whip. I remember that in a rage he slammed one of my cousins, who was only three, against a tree. I was fourteen. Beast!, I said to

him. We never spoke again. I couldn't really give a damn about
the rest of the family either. At the time I went into hiding in
their house with Julián, after I returned to Spain, they did take me
in, but they neatly listed all the outgoings for laundry and food
and deducted them from the thirty thousand pesetas, which were
due to me as inheritance. And of course they then sent the
money to Fernando, although I was the beneficiary, women didn't
count for them.

Marga said, what's past is past, and it's not the children's fault.
That was just like her, my sister. Always concerned to be concil-
iatory. Julián says she was very pretty and was always smiling. I was
pretty too. Only I've been a feminist all my life, it would never
have occurred to me to load myself with jewellery. At the age of
twelve I pushed all the junk – rings, bracelets, necklaces – across
the table to my mother and said, get rid of it, I'm not a cow that
has to be adorned, so that it gets a good price at the cattle market.

We got a friendly welcome in Minorca. I liked the island right
away. Decades later we bought a plot of land with my mother's
inheritance; in the early '80s we had a house built. Since then I
visit our relations once a year. They're very discreet, very taciturn.
I don't know if that's true of all Minorcans, but I do think it's
typical of the inhabitants of the island, they don't talk much.
Pleasant, but reserved people. My uncle and aunts are not to
blame for the behaviour of their parents, who let my mother
down, back then. So I never talk about it.

My grandfather died in the early 1960s. After the war he was
Communist council leader in Favoriten for a couple of months.

Then he worked in Feichtenbach, as warden of a children's convalescent home of the city of Vienna. He was relieved of the post
in 1950. He drew a small pension until he died.

I sometimes visited him and his wife. Come again soon, they
said, when I left. But I didn't go often. Because I felt that it hurt
my mother. Although she never discouraged me, on the contrary,
she said: Well, if you want to, then go. She had one or two
admirers, nothing serious, at least not on her side. I have a feeling
it was because of me she didn't want to marry again. She was
always there for me, until her death, in 1986. Was my father her
great love? Oh, I think so. But above all he was her great
disappointment.

In May '68, under de Gaulle, the centre of Paris was seething with
unrest. For the first time people stopped in the streets, debated
with one another, stood up vociferously and emphatically for
their opinions, also changed them in the course of the discussions. There were mass meetings, the ruling class felt threatened.
On the other hand the revolt remained a game, that was soon
clear to me. Because I saw that the police didn't intervene as the
demonstrators built barricades in the streets, five or six barricades
as high as a man in a single night, on the 10th or 8th of May. I've
been on many protest marches in my life, against the war in
Algeria, for example, where during a single demonstration, thirteen people were killed, so I know, that if they're serious the
police can clear any square and any street in next to no time. I
asked myself why the police forces allowed stones to be thrown
at them, why they only fired tear gas grenades and used water
cannon, why they hesitated so long, why they proceeded almost
cautiously. I concluded that the rebellious students were children

of the bourgeoisie, they didn't want to club them down, and they didn't club them down. But it was a nice piece of theatre.

I took part. I was criticised by the Communists as a factionalist and an ultra-left adventurer because of it. I defended myself against these accusations, a Communist, I said, has to be on the side of the masses.

What was interesting was the cultural shift. The change in mentality. At the universities the professors lost a little bit of their absolute power. Before that, at the Sorbonne all the students had to stand up when a professor entered the lecture theatre, a couple even clapped, we were only allowed to sit down after the professors had permitted us to. It was also not permissible to address them just like that. I remember I was once in a pissoir, and a professor came in. He passed water beside me, and I committed the crime of speaking to him. He was beside himself. How dare you! Who do you think you are! One doesn't address a professor in the toilet.

After the street battles manners became more relaxed, that was progress. Feminism too was positive. But there was no revolution in sight. It was all very romantic, like a revival of a nineteenth-century social upheaval, with cobblestones and red flags and all seven verses of the 'International'. And it was also dangerous. I think that if the Communist Party had not stayed on the sidelines, if it had joined the movement or even taken power, then there would have been a bloodbath.

To my mother 1968 was the year of the great disappointment. She was convinced that a radical change was imminent. Likewise my uncle, who died soon after. They didn't understand the caution of the French Party. That it was unable to take advantage of the auspicious moment. That view was very widespread among the Spaniards. A young man, a Spanish comrade, who had fled to

Paris, cursed us, because we didn't take a leading part in the May revolt. To me he was a Trotskyist.

I never had anything to do with Communists. After the war I was briefly a member of the Free Austrian Youth, but that was more for the girls. Through my mother I was a Social Democrat. I still am. Ultimately it turned out, in the states of the Eastern Bloc, that Communism wasn't the right way, to put it mildly.

I rarely think of my father. Now more than earlier, that comes with age. During the big political events like the Hungarian Uprising, the Prague Spring or the collapse of the Soviet Union he did come to mind: What does he think about it. What would his attitude be. Is he embittered.

My parents were happy that after Franco's death they were able to travel to Spain again. When I began to study, they had hoped I would later settle in the land of their ancestors, like many children of émigrés. But when I married a French woman and remained in Paris, they discarded the idea of returning permanently to Spain. But it became the only place they went on holiday, and once they had got some money together, they bought an apartment in Cullera, a seaside resort near Valencia. They even participated in the activities of the local Party organisation, went to the meetings of their section and sold the Party newspaper. All their commitment wasn't worth the effort. It was sad for me to see, towards the end of her life, my mother losing all her illusions, as she was forced to realise that while the Spanish people welcomed the freedom they had regained, they weren't interested in politics. But the worst thing was that after the illusions she lost her memories too.

There is still no cure for Creutzfeld-Jakob disease. At that time it was supposed to be caused by a virus, today we know that prions are responsible. The proteins bring about breakdown symptoms in the brain and in motor activity beginning with sleep and memory disorders, followed later on by changes in personality structure. The outbreak of the illness is not predictable. On average, say the doctors, it affects one in every two million people. My mother was that one.

In August 1987 in Cullera her condition suddenly worsened, so that she had to be brought back by plane. It was no longer possible to have a conversation with her, she seemed to be far away, stared into space. My stepfather was in despair. He simply couldn't bear her not responding to anything any more.

I first noticed Margarita's illness here in Madrid. I had to have a cataract operation, and she came from Paris to help out with the housework. I right away found her a little strange, but I couldn't see very well without glasses. On the first day she went shopping with Fernando. After that she had to rest immediately. She was completely exhausted. And then it took her three hours to fry a fish, three hours to do something that should have taken ten minutes. She mixed up the cutlery, wanted to eat the soup with her fork. She was tired all the time. Hardly had she sat down somewhere than her eyelids drooped. We didn't argue. But before she left, she said, I'll never forget what you once said to me. That I have my mother on my conscience.

Marga is buried in the cemetery at Créteil. On the gravestone it says:

Margarita Ferrer
1916–1987

The grave is closed with a marble slab. On the slab there is an open stone book. On the left hand-page are chiselled a rose and five letters: MARGA. On the right-hand page are the words:

Jamás
Te olvidaré
Paco

'I will never forget you.' He survived her by just less than five years.

Go on! I want to know everything.
   – That is everything now.
   – She didn't talk about me any more?
   – She didn't talk about anyone any more.
   – Then she did forget me.
   – He says she felt guilty all her life. Guilty towards you. That's what you want to hear, isn't it.
   – Why guilty.
   – Because, at the end of the Civil War, you saw the chance of emigrating to Mexico. She was against it, because she didn't want to leave her mother behind. So you stayed too. That's why, she said, everything happened as it did. And something else. Edi says, Suárez really wanted to adopt him. She didn't allow that.

— Because of me?

— Yes. It was her wish that he would always bear your name.

I married young, at twenty. The child was already on the way, a boy. We called him Rudolf, after my father. Why, is hard to explain. It was an inner impulse. Neither he nor my stepson, whom my second wife brought to the marriage, have ever shown any interest in the world of their grandfather. Perhaps that's my fault. I didn't want to push them in a particular direction. I imagined, sooner or later the children would realise what counts in life.

A couple of years ago I was at a psychology congress. There was another Friemel, apart from me, on the list of participants. At the same time I ordered tickets for the ferry to Minorca. The travel agency sent them to me with the wrong first name, that of the other Friemel at the congress. I think he was a man of the same age as me. I didn't have him pointed out to me, I didn't approach him, I didn't speak to him.

I don't mean to say that I rejected my family history. I just didn't take an interest in it, because I always had the feeling it was not something my mother really wanted, even if she never explicitly said so. I didn't make an effort. And with the death of my grandfather there was no link any more anyway. Now there would also be language problems as well. I wouldn't even be able to communicate with my half-brother. Nevertheless, I would like to get to know him. My heart would be pounding.

I've often asked myself why I don't want to find out anything about Rudi, about his youth in Vienna, about the relatives in Vienna, nothing about the Spaniards of Mauthausen, nothing about my parents' friends in Paris. I'm not in contact with any of them any more. Perhaps it's a way of protecting myself. I bear a scar, which must not be allowed to open.

6

THE SHIRT

On the morning of 30th December 1944 Himmler's dispatch, granting the request, reached the camp commandant. In the course of the morning the five gallows were put up for the third time.

– Return to quarters was at 4 pm, the usual command then was: Fall in for roll call, for which we had to form up in fives in front of the huts, then: Dismiss, go and get supper. But that evening we waited in vain for the command to dismiss. We, the fifteen thousand prisoners of the men's camp.

– As usual the condemned men were examined by the doctor, to see if their state of health was able to cope with the coming excitement, and as usual the doctor came to a positive conclusion.

– The SS, who never missed such a spectacle, also turned up.

– Then the five men were dragged out of the bunker of Block 11. They were wearing only shirt and trousers and despite the cold were barefoot.

– Heads held high, even though chalk-white, the unfortunates strode to the roll call square, which was lit up by searchlights.

– The whole way they shouted political slogans. They were being hit all the time, but didn't stop shouting.

– Each of them was placed in front of a gallows. Diagonally behind the gallows was the Christmas tree, a huge fir, which towered above everything else. The electric candles were on. The prisoners' commander read the order which had been approved in Berlin. Accordingly the Polish detainees Piotr Piaty and Bernard Swiercyzna and the Reich German detainees Ernst Burger, Rudolf Friemel and Ludwig Vesely were sentenced to death by hanging for attempted escape, diversionary activities and contact with partisans. The order was to be put into effect immediately.

– Even before the camp commander had given the signal to carry out the death sentence, Piaty and Swierczyna stood up straight and shouted across the wide square, so loudly that they could be heard in the furthest corner: *Niech zyje Polska! Niech zyje wolnosc! Long live Poland! Long live freedom!* The Nazi thugs fell on the two of them, dragged them to the gallows and even now continued hitting them with fists and rifle butts.

– I had to stand about three paces away. I saw how in their anger the SS men lost all self-control. Boger and Kaduk maltreated those who were already hanging. They struck them in the face, kicked them and pulled them by their feet.

– I was standing further back. I couldn't hear so well. But I think I saw one of them kick the SS man in front of him in the face and himself slip his head into the noose and immediately jump.

– At that moment Ernst Burger shouted: Down with Fascism! Long live a free, independent Austria! And Rudi Friemel raised his bound hands above his head and shouted: Down with the brown murderers! Long live——. His words died away in a wheezing, as an SS man threw the noose over his head. Then it was young Vesely's turn. His last words were: Today us, tomorrow you.

– I think it was Rudi who shouted: Today us, tomorrow you! The four others shouted: Long live Poland, Austria, the Red Army. The SS chief clerk, his face red with anger, beat them with his whip.

– It was a feeling of humiliation, of shame and powerlessness: You can't do anything. You think they're looking you straight in the eye. I felt that Rudi, who was standing quite close to me, was looking me straight in the eye. Then the box under his feet was kicked away, the rope tautened, the body twitched for a few seconds, I still saw the tongue getting long and longer, the staring eyes, then I couldn't make anything out any more.

– All the prisoners who had fallen in, took off their caps after the execution.

– There's one thing I forgot to say: They were wearing old trousers and worn-out shirts, only Rudi wasn't. Heinz Dürmayer, the camp elder, had arranged for the shirt he had worn at his wedding to be brought to him. I don't know if it was Rudi's last wish. I only know that he was hanged in his wedding shirt, the one embroidered with roses. His wife, the Spanish woman, never knew.

7

AFTERWARDS AND BEFORE

The survivor, who shortly before his planned escape in August 1944 is transferred to Neuengamme Concentration Camp, so that it is only after his liberation in May '45 that he finds out about Rudi's death, and who takes note of the information, which hits him hard, in the Auschwitz way, as he says: It's happened, there's no use whining about it, and who in Vienna, soon after his return, gives a lecture about Auschwitz, so that the world finally knows the whole truth... and so on.

A young woman who comes up to him, after he has finished the lecture, and asks him, if by chance he knew a certain Rudi Friemel in the camp.

He, the survivor, who nods.

She, who asks: What has happened to Rudi.

He, who replies: That Friemel was hanged on the roll call square at the end of December the previous year.

The young woman (whom the survivor has never seen before and whom he will never meet again), who collapses weeping uncontrollably.

The brother of the survivor, who assists the young woman, helps her to her feet, leads her away, entrusts her to the care of others and then reproaches the survivor, because he treated the woman so roughly: Have you no heart, no soul!

And again and definitively the survivor, who responds:

Anyone who was in Auschwitz has a callus on his soul for the rest of his life.

Franz Danimann, Marina Ferrer Rey, Édouard Friemel, Norbert Friemel, Kurt Hacker, Ferdinand Hackl, Hans Landauer, Hermann Langbein, Josef Meisel, Dagmar Ostermann, Alois Peter, Erich Wolf. These are the names of those who have trusted me with their memories. Seven of them have died in the meantime. Leopold Spira, who entrusted this story to me, is also dead, as is Francisco Comellas, who was the first to help me on, and Fernando Escribano Checa, the engaging and reticent man at Marina's side.

The Auschwitz Museum and the Dokumentationsarchiv des österreichischen Widerstandes (Archive of Austrian Resistance) made the statements of the former prisoners Jan Dziopka, Stanislaw Klodzinski, Viktor Lederer, Erwin Olszowka, Ludwig Soswinski and Alfred Woycicki, among others, available to me. Likewise helpful to me were the documents in the Archiv österreichischer Spanienkämpfer (Archive of Austrian Veterans of Spain), established by Hans Landauer, the information provided by Julián Escribano Ferrer, and the relevant works by Hermann Langbein, Danuta Czech and Lore Shelley. A selection of stories by Tadeusz Borowski is published in English under the title This Way for the Gas, Ladies and Gentlemen *translated by Barbara Vedder (Penguin Books, New York 1976). Jenny Spritzer's account* Ich war Nr. 10291. Als Sekretärin in Auschwitz *(I was No. 10291. A Secretary in Auschwitz) is published by Rothenhäusler Verlag. In it there is a picture with the following caption: 'It is reckoned that by the year 2010 there will be no more Auschwitz survivors.' It is not only because of the wrong date that I refuse to believe this prediction.*